Squod spent the [illegible]
did, being a good [illegible]
customers in a drink. When his son came home, the landlord of the Black Lion was in his usual state.

"Ah, Father, look at you. Once again, you're your own best customer." The lad had learned to speak properly at the theater.

Squod staggered to his feet and pulled his son aside. "Them detectives were here earlier, and they wants to talk to ya. They wants to know if ya was mixed up wi' that there Little Liz. I were a wee drunk last night, but I thinks I knows more than I wants to. Just 'cause your mum walked out on us, it don't mean all women, even them tarts, is so bad. Does ya understand me, Jack?"

The door of the taproom banged open, and Blathers strode in, followed by Duff. "We wishes ta talk wi' your lad, Squod." Jack Squod jumped from his chair and dashed into the back room. He ripped out a back door and went over the fence.

"We only wants ta talk wi' him. Where's he goin'?" By the time Blathers and Duff realized the boy was running away and began pursuit, young Jack was lost in the dank, dark, dangerous maze that was nineteenth-century London.

****

From time to time, over the years, the corpses of "professional ladies" decorated the brothels, sordid inns, and slimiest street corners of London. Except for the occasional arrest of an angry pimp, the murders went unsolved. A Jack of Spades was often found at the scene.

Tales of the Black Lion

by

Michael B. Coyle

This is a work of fiction. Names, characters, places, and incidents are either the product of the author's imagination or are used fictitiously, and any resemblance to actual persons living or dead, business establishments, events, or locales, is entirely coincidental.

Tales of the Black Lion

Contact Information: info@thewildrosepress.com

Cover Art by *Debbie Taylor*

The Wild Rose Press, Inc.
PO Box 708
Adams Basin, NY 14410-0708
Visit us at www.thewildrosepress.com

Publishing History
First Mainstream Historical Rose Edition, 2015
Print ISBN 978-1-5092-0372-7
Digital ISBN 978-1-5092-0373-4

Published in the United States of America

Dedication

To Kathe, my wife,
and Katie and Jeanne, my daughters

Acknowledgements

Thanks to several of my first readers, Chris Ashton, Pam Hood, Sally Crosiar, and Jeannie Crain.

I also want to thank my good friends at the Canandaigua Writers Group, at the Wood Library. They are all great writers who help me believe that I am a writer, too.

Another great source of encouragement has been the Colgate Writers Conference. Thanks to Matt Leone, Cody Tipton, and the great writers Dana Spiotta and Paul Cody.

Finally, without the help of the kindly and erudite editor Nan Swanson this would not be a book.

TALE ONE

One Murder at the Black Lion
February 1837

Murder most factious!

Chapter One

"Tell your gov'nor that Blathers and Duff is here, will you?"

"'E's up the stairs, guardin' the room, so's not to 'ave the scene disturbed."

The detectives looked up the tilted stairway toward the second floor.

The sign at the front of the building showed a black lion couchant, bearing in his dexter paw a Maltese Cross. It said the inn was "Est. 1730." The stairway had celebrated its centennial a few years past. It showed worn spots caused by boots climbing up and down all those years. The building had settled and tilted, taking the stairway with it.

The shorter, stouter, shaggier man said, "Mind that there loose board, Duff."

At the top of this hundred-year monument, the landlord had placed himself in front of a door. He held his arms folded tightly over his chest, about halfway between his burgeoning belly and his purple-veined nose.

"We is Blathers and Duff from the Metropolitan Police. I'm Blathers, and this here is Duff." He pointed to the tall, skinny person who followed him up the stairs. "What's the situation here, then?" Blathers was the spokesman for the detective duo.

“There’s been a bloody murder, hasn’t there. See fer yarselves.” The landlord released his grip on himself, turned, and opened the door.

The scene was bloody, all right.

Duff’s practiced eye estimated the room to be about twenty feet by thirty feet, although, like the rest of the ancient inn, it was not perfectly plumb. In the center sat a large pine table. It fit the room in a way that allowed for benches on each side. The bench, which should have been at a shorter end of the table, to the right of Blathers and Duff as they entered the room, had been tossed aside, against the adjacent wall.

At that end of the table lay the body of a young woman, legs bent over the edge at the knees, feet dangling above the floor.

“’Tis just as I found her. No ’un has been in the room t’day ’cept me. I sends for ya as soon as I discovers her. I’s been standin’ guard here at the door e’r since.”

Her throat had been slashed. From one angle, it looked like she had a second, very bloody, mouth. Blood covered the tabletop. Some had run down each leg and dripped from her heels onto the floor. Two dark red pools had formed. The girl looked to be in her late teens. She was almost naked. Several stab wounds were visible on her exposed breast. Her tattered skirt hung on the displaced bench. Blood-soaked underwear clung to her thighs. Slashes in her legs and stomach contributed more blood to the ghastly sight.

“What’s it they calls ya, Landlord?” Blathers asked while Duff surveyed the room. The detectives were used to blood-spattered corpses and the smell of death.

“Phil Squod.”

"Duff, are ya done looking round here?"

"I am." The boney detective's Adam's apple bounced in his neck.

"Mr. Squod, does ya has a key to this here door?"

"I does."

"Then why don't you lock it? Then ya won't be havin' ta stand round here for the rest of your bloody life, will ya. We can have our little chat about what it is has happened here down in your lovely taproom." Squod locked the door, and they all plodded down the tilted stairway.

"I'll have a bit o' brandy," Blathers said. "It's a wee too early for me to be 'joyin' an ale, but there's a chill in the air."

"Tea for me, please." Any time of day was too early for Duff to partake of intoxicating drinks.

Squod didn't know he had offered refreshments, but went off to secure the drinks without comment. When he returned, he had a pint of ale for himself. The three sat at a small pine table near the fireplace. Glowing logs eased the dampness of the morning.

Blathers downed his brandy in one swig, wiped the back of his hand across his mouth, and said, "Now then, tell us all about it."

Squod gripped his pint with both hands. "I have no idear what happened, do I. There were a private party in that there room last night, but I were busy wi' other customers. We had quite the crowd last night, we did. My girl, Jane, took care o' the party. It were a special cel'bration among them writer and actor types. A bir'day party, I believes."

"Does ya know the name of the poor girl upstairs?"

"I doesn't, but I has seen her on the streets at

times."

"Is Jane the girl we saw as we came in?" Duff asked.

"Oh, no, that's Sally. She's here to help wi' them what comes in fer their noon meal. Jane does fer the even' folk."

Duff asked another question. "How is it the writers and actors chose your establishment for their party, Mr. Squod?"

"It's me son, Jack. He acts down at the playhouse. He knows all 'em actors and writers, and he brought 'em in, didn't he."

"Were he a part o' the party?" Blathers regained control of the interrogation.

"He were at the start, but he were performin', and he were required to go out early. He left while the early drinkin' were goin' on."

"Is actin' your son's only work, then?"

"Oh, no, Jack helps out around here wi' the cuttin'o' the meats and the cookin'."

"Who was the guests?"

"I don't right know. Jane would know. 'Em young men sure love her, doesn't they."

"We'll be needin' ta talk ta her, then. Where do she live?"

"Just down the alley. Sally'll fetch 'er fer ya."

Squod told Sally to go for Jane.

"Afore you go, Sally girl, I'll be havin' a wee bit more brandy." The chill continued to bother Blathers.

Sally brought Blathers another drink, more tea for Duff, and headed out the door. Five minutes later she was back with Jane in tow.

"You're wantin' to talk to me?" Jane had neatly

combed blond hair. A full skirt partially disguised shapely hips. Beneath the skirt one could see lovely ankles that hinted at lovely legs. Her beautiful face featured big blue eyes, soft pink skin, and heart-shaped mouth. Duff admired her sweet face. Blathers admired the fact she was "buxom."

Blathers began. "There's been a murder. A young woman is stabbed and sprawlin' on the table in the room above. They're sayin' ya might be the one to tell us about it."

"I knows nothin'. Honest, mister. I seen her come into the party, and I knowed there was to be trouble, so I skedaddled."

"How did you know there would be trouble?" Duff asked.

"Every time one o' them whores shows up there's trouble. Them men are all alike. When they brought her in I says to meself, this is it, and I takes me leave. Whores is bad business anywhere. They does nothing but lead men to the devil."

"What time were it that she arrived?" Blathers asked.

"Were 'bout half ten, I guess."

"And who was the gents what was remaining when you left?"

"Well, there were Mr. Dickens. Ya' know, the writer."

"Ah, Pickwick!" Duff knew the name.

"That's the feller. And his good friend Mr. Forster. There were a couple of others I doesn't know as well as I knows Mr. Dickens and Mr. Forster. Them two comes round here quite often, and always asks fer me ta serve 'em."

Duff made a note of the two names and asked, "So the girl was still alive when you left the inn?"

"I swears she were, sir."

"Was Mr. Squod's son, Jack, at the party when you left?"

"Jack weren't there. I doesn't know where he were. He could ha' been anywhere. Maybe he were out getting more whores fer the party."

"How did the gentlemen get their drinks after you left?" Duff continued.

"I guesses they just fetched for themselves, sir."

Duff turned to the landlord, "Did you know Jane had left, Mr. Squod? And if so, did you serve any drinks to the upstairs room?"

"I did not. I were busy wi' me other customers. Likes I says afore, I had no'in' to do wi' any goin's on outside the taproom."

Chapter Two

Charles Dickens was perched on a stool behind the stage at Drury Lane Theater. “Well, aren’t you a couple of colorful characters. I’ll have to remember you two. What can I do for you?”

Blathers and Duff didn’t know how to respond to this young upstart, who was quickly developing the reputation of being one of the most clever men in London. Blathers just cleared his throat and got down to business. “We’re investigatin’ murder, and we believes you may has been involved.”

“I haven’t been involved in any murder of which I am aware, but you have piqued my interest. Tell me more.”

“There were a party last night at the Black Lion. It ’pears at the end o’ the night a woman were killed by havin’ her throat cut. We has been informed you was ’tendin’ at the party.”

“I was. It was a party to celebrate my twenty-fifth birthday, but what girl had her throat cut? Not sweet Jane.”

“’Twas the girl what was doin’ the entertainin’ for ya gents, if ya calls that entertainin’.”

“Well, when I left, that girl was alive and well. Very well and very, very alive, from what I could see.”

Duff asked, “Were there other girls at the party,

Mr. Dickens?"

"The only other girl was the lovely Jane. Ah, what a lovely ass-pect her smile is. But, come to think of it, I didn't see her at all after the young tart showed up. I meant to see that she got a generous tip."

"Who else was in attendance when the girl arrived?" Duff was usually more grammatically correct than his partner. He was very particular in the presence of the celebrated writer.

"There was myself and Mr. Forster, John Forster. We, however, left together shortly after the girl came in. Not our type of entertainment, you know. Let me see. When we left, Mr. Stanfield, Mr. Maclise, Mr. Cruikshank, Mr. Macready, and Mr. Thackeray, that is Mr. William Makepeace Thackeray, were still present."

Duff jotted down the names and asked, "Who brought in the girl?"

"She must have been sent up from downstairs. Perhaps that young Squod fellow had a hand in it. He was always trying to ingratiate himself to my friends and me."

"You means the young actor?" Blathers asked.

"Well, he isn't much of an actor, but that's the fellow, yes."

"Was he there at the party, then?"

"He was there early on, to be certain the arrangements were in order, but he left. I didn't see him again. Said he had some job at the theater, but the play was over by the time Forster and I left the party, and he had not returned."

"What's the kind of a fellow is this here lad? His name be Jack, is that right?"

"Yes, Jack. He's a quiet fellow. Really loves the

theater. Too bad he's not a better actor. Well he may learn."

Duff took up his pencil again and asked, "Can you give us some idea where we can find the other gentlemen you named?"

Dickens provided information on the most likely place to locate each of the members of the party, and the detectives set out to continue their investigation.

****

Blathers and Duff started with John Forster. He was Dickens' best friend. "Indeed, Dickens and I left together shortly after the entertainment of ill repute arrived."

The two detectives interviewed the other members of the party over the course of the afternoon. The conclusion derived from their testimony was that each had left while the young lady was fully clothed, and, except for being quite drunk, was in good health. That is, they all had left except William Makepeace Thackeray. He remained behind to settle the bill. Yes, as far as they knew, the girl was still present.

Chapter Three

Thackeray submitted to an interview. "I was appointed treasurer for the evening. I usually am. Perhaps I am the most sober among them. They are clever fellows, and I enjoy their company, although sometimes their lowbred habits come out when they have been drinking. I always collect a sufficient amount to cover the costs before the drinking begins. Quite naturally, I remained to the last to settle up with the house.

"The girl was passed out in the room when I went downstairs to locate the landlord. The sot was so inebriated that he could hardly stand. He had no idea how much we owed. The girl who waited on us, apparently a close friend of Dickens and Forster, had vacated the premises.

"I gave the landlord what I thought was fair and left my card with instructions for him to contact me if he felt he had been shorted. It is unlikely he will even remember the conversation. I then left the horrible place without returning to the upstairs room. Is there anything else you gentlemen wish to know?"

Blathers asked, "Does ya know who were servin' drinks after Jane left?"

"I guess I wasn't paying attention. I never drink after my meal. Perhaps the serving girl returned, or perhaps it was that foolish young actor, the landlord's son. I thought I saw him in the taproom as I was leaving. If that is all, good day, gentlemen." Mr. William Makepeace Thackeray dismissed Blathers and Duff.

****

The questioning of Mr. Dickens and his associates took all of the afternoon. By the time Mr. Thackeray completed his concise statement, it was nearing five o'clock. "I believes we has a bit o' time to stop back at the Black Lion," Blathers said. The chill was still in the air, and a little brandy along with a pint of bitter would warm the bones and revive the spirits. Duff agreed because he had discovered the tea at the Black Lion was well brewed, even if the customers were ill bred.

But it wasn't only the thought of warming beverages that motivated the detective duo to return to the inn. They both, in their own way, had a feeling there was more to be learned from Phil Squod and his family and friends.

"I thinks we needs ta talk wi' that young Squod."

While Blathers was hitching up the horse, Duff asked, "Do you think Squod was telling all of the truth?"

Blathers climbed into the gig. "The only one I believes o' all o' them are that Mr. Dickens feller. Ho, Pincher, geddyup."

When they arrived, they found Mr. Dickens and Mr. Forster ensconced in chairs before the fire, each with a brandy in hand. "Ah, the detectives. How does your investigation go?" Dickens asked.

"We is still in the midst o' the inquires."

Squod was tending to his customers in the taproom.

"Well we has cleaned up the scene o' the crime, hasn't we," he said. "The parish has sent o'er the un'ertaker 'bout noon, and I has two chars up there scrubbin' away e'er since. That there room is valuable space t' me. It's not only fer parties. When we has an overflow o' lodgers, we put mattresses on the table fer sleepin'."

"Well, I for one am happy I didn't know that when I was dining last evening," Forster said.

Dickens laughed at Forster's pretense of squeamishness. "By the time you got around to food, John, it looked like you would be taking your meal on your hands and knees off the floor." Forster raised his arms in the air and wrinkled his brow.

"So the crime scene has been 'rased, has it? Well, never mind. Duff here has seen it, and it is now stored in his mind's eye. He remembers all he sees."

"Yes," Duff said. "I remember there was a playing card stuck to the table with blood. It was the Knave of Spades. It was plastered right there between the girl's legs."

Blather asked, "Was there card playin' at your party, Mr. Dickens?"

Dickens smiled and glanced at Forster. "Now what would a party be without cards, Mr. Blathers? By the way, Mr. Duff, the Knave is now more commonly called the Jack."

"Right you are, Mr. Dickens, I remember now, it's called the Jack, but what happened to the remainder of the deck?"

"Damned if I know," Dickens answered. "Perhaps the killer just left the Jack as a kind of calling card."

Blathers asked for another brandy, and Duff asked for tea. "You hasn't yet paid for the drinks ya had earlier or these here in front o' ya," Squod said.

"Mr. Squod, we is present on these here premises on business. An' part o' that business is ta look after the good name o' your 'stablishment. Certainly ya wishes to remain in our good graces." Blathers glared at the landlord, thinking how bold he was to even suggest he and Duff should pay for their drinks.

"I'll stand the gentlemen's beverages," Dickens announced.

Blathers said, "Ah, that's very decent of you, sir. But never you mind, I is sure that Mr. Squod were makin' a little joke, and always meant fer our drinks ta be at the compliments o' the house." The landlord simply nodded his consent.

"We has stopped by with a few additional questions for you, Mr. Squod." Blathers, after receiving his free brandy, thought he should, at least, deal with a small amount of business. "Has the victim been identified?"

"She has," Squod said. "The un'ertaker knows her, and she is on the parish records. Her name be Lizabeth Stride, but on the street they calls her as Little Liz."

Duff stroked his long thin chin. "Do we understand your son knew her, Mr. Squod?"

"I don't believes so. Me son is still quite young, only nineteen, and he don't mix wi' the likes o' that tart."

"Can we speak with your son?" Duff asked.

"'He ain't on these here premises at this time. I'm not sure when he'll be back."

"Good enough, then," Blathers said, draining his glass. "We'll stops back another time."

Chapter Four

Squod spent the rest of the evening as he always did, being a good host and joining most of his customers in a drink. When his son came home, the landlord of the Black Lion was in his usual state.

"Ah, Father, look at you. Once again, you're your own best customer." The lad had learned to speak properly at the theater.

Squod staggered to his feet and pulled his son aside. "Them detectives were here earlier, and they wants to talk to ya. They wants to know if ya was mixed up wi' that there Little Liz. I were a wee drunk last night, but I thinks I knows more than I wants to. Just 'cause your mum walked out on us, it don't mean all women, even them tarts, is so bad. Does ya understand me, Jack?"

The door of the taproom banged open, and Blathers strode in, followed by Duff. "We wishes ta talk wi' your lad, Squod." Jack Squod jumped from his chair and dashed into the back room. He ripped out a back door and went over the fence.

"We only wants ta talk wi' him. Where's he goin'?" By the time Blathers and Duff realized the boy was running away and began pursuit, young Jack was lost in the dank, dark, dangerous maze that was nineteenth-century London.

****

From time to time, over the years, the corpses of "professional ladies" decorated the brothels, sordid inns, and slimiest street corners of London. Except for the occasional arrest of an angry pimp, the murders went unsolved. A Jack of Spades was often found at the scene.

TALE TWO

Two Detectives Aid a Lady
November 1841

The play's the thing wherein
they catch the enemy of the Queen.

Chapter 1

Blathers and I had not visited the Black Lion for some time. In fact, the old inn had been closed for several years and only recently reopened under new management. Blathers suggested that we stop for old times' sake. We entered the taproom, where there were only two other patrons. One was saying, "Here, Forster, have a seat near the fire. It's a blasted cold and damp evening." Charles Dickens pulled a pine bench away from a table and slid it closer to the blaze on the hearth. "Jane, bring those brandies over here in the warmth, will you?" The buxom young serving girl brought a tumbler to each of the men where they slouched on the bench in front of the fire. I saw Mr. Dickens pat the girl's backside when she set the drinks on a nearby table.

Blathers said, "Evening, gents."

"My word, my two favorite detectives," Mr. Dickens called out. "It's been some time since we have seen you. Come join us for a drink. You recall Mr. Forster?"

"Aye, we do. Good evening, Mr. Forster." My short, round partner extended his hand to Forster, then shook Mr. Dickens' hand. I followed, shaking the hand of both the celebrated writer and his best friend.

"Indeed, it's Blathers and Duff, is it not?"

"Blathers and Duff we is, Mr. Forster." As usual, Blathers acted as our spokesman.

Mr. Dickens said, "Well, sit down, gentlemen. What will you have to drink? Jane, a little attention, if you please."

"I'll have a brandy, thank ya, Mr. Dickens. I'm sure Duff will have his tea, seein' he don't partake o' potent beverages."

"That's correct, I'll have tea, thank you, Mr. Dickens." As I answered I pulled another bench in front of the fire. Jane delivered the drinks. This time Mr. Forster patted her derriere. She smiled an appreciative smile. I believe she expected to go home with a generous tip at the end of evening.

"We're celebrating another successful production at Drury Lane," the author announced.

I asked, "Is that Sam Weller in your play? He is quite a fellow, in your Pickwick writings." I wanted Mr. Dickens to know I was a fan. "Pickwick is lucky to have someone like Sam. I think quite a few of us depend on a good partner to keep us out of trouble, the way Mr. Pickwick depends on Sam." I glanced at Blathers, hoping he would get my point. "Don't you agree, Blathers?"

Blathers ignored me. Mr. Dickens smiled and shook his head.

Mr. Forster changed the subject. "Squod has sold the place, then?" he said.

Mr. Dickens said, "He has. After it turned out his son Jack was accused of the bloody murder that took place upstairs, he could no longer face his patrons. The service suffered, and the customers went elsewhere."

Mr. Forster placed his right index finger along the

side of his nose in a thoughtful manner. "Indeed, he hardly ever saw anyone, anyway. He could look you right in the eye, but he was always so drunk, he would never remember you were there."

Mr. Dickens nodded, "It was a shame. The Black Lion was a grand establishment. We used to drink here often." He and his friend appeared quite comfortable in the taproom of the old inn. "We can hope the improvements the new owners are making will last."

"Indeed, I agree." Then Forster changed the subject again. "Wasn't it a fine turnout for the play tonight? I think we have a great hit on our hands. We should make a pretty penny from this one."

"I see the Iron Duke was in attendance, accompanied by his political friend Sir Robert Peel and another dandy whom I didn't recognize."

"Ah, that was Wellington's cousin, Percy Wesley. Indeed, he's been seen around town in the Duke's company for several weeks now. One always wonders when Tories like Wellington and Peel are together, but this addition of the cousin to the mix is certainly mysterious."

Dickens turned to us, "Well, now that the Bow Street Runners are no more, are you two with the Metropolitan Police? If you're back here to nab Jack Squod, you are out of luck. Since old man Squod has sold out, it's unlikely the young one will ever come in here again. We understand a Mr. and Mrs. Barkis are now running the place. Although, as you can see, the lovely Jane is back to serve in the evenings."

"Yes," Forster added, "and the place smells so much better than it did when that sot Squod was in charge. It is not only a more pleasant place to drink, but

I would even consider taking a meal here again."

Dickens said, "Forster, when you are sober you are such a prude. Have another brandy, quickly, please." Forster smiled, wrinkled his forehead, downed the remainder of his drink, and signaled for another.

Blathers quelled the joviality with his serious countenance. "Ta answer your question, Mr. Dickens, as ya knows, the Runners has been disbanded fer some time now. Sir Robert Peel has founded his Metropolitan Police Force at Scotland Yard and folded the Runners into that."

I added, "We did stay on with the police for some time, and always considered ourselves to be still with the Runners, but as Runners, we made our living off the rewards we were paid. The detectives at the Yard are now forbidden to take any rewards, and the pay is slight."

"My goodness, that means you gentlemen are without visible means of support," Dickens quipped. "Good show Forster and I are here to stand your drinks."

"Ah, we has both taken some temporary 'ployment. But thank ya fer the beverages just the same," Blathers said.

"What employment?"

"We is both acting as porters fer…"

"The Society for the Suppression of Vice," I completed the statement. Blathers always called our employers the Vice Ladies.

"Can ya 'magine that, helpin' them white chokers and fat old women bust up bookshops just 'cause they don't like the dirty words in some o' them books. It's a sad day when the pride o' London's detectives is reduced ta a thin' like that."

"But it pays good." I said. "We would be pleased to stand you and Mr. Forster a beverage, Mr. Dickens. Jane, if you please, another round of drinks, on Mr. Blathers and me."

Blathers glared at me. Life had changed substantially. As police neither of us had ever paid for a drink. He didn't take well to change, particularly when it affected his pocketbook.

Jane delivered the drinks. I paid her, but I certainly refrained from touching any portion of her anatomy. And I didn't feel a tip was necessary.

Both Mr. Dickens and Mr. Forster expressed their thanks. Dickens asked, "Well, what's your plan?"

"We is thinkin' o' becomin' private detectives. People could hire us ta recover their stolen jewels and like that."

Just then, a very large woman entered the room. She looked like a female "John Bull." She had a bright red face, and her sizable bust counterbalanced an equally sizeable behind. I thought that a diminishing of the bulk of either her front or her rear would have thrown her off balance.

"You're Mr. Dickens, the writer. I just love that Sam Weller." Everybody in London loved Sam. He was the character that made Dickens a character.

"Mrs. Barkis, I presume? May I present my dear friend Mr. Forster, and these gentlemen are Blathers and Duff, the detectives."

"Pleased to make your acquaintance, gentlemen. Welcome to the Black Lion. My given name is Clara. Please be free to call me Clara."

Mr. Forster said, "Indeed, you have made

remarkable improvements in the old place. That sot Squod had let it go terrible."

"Well, thank you for your comments. Me and Barkis is trying our best."

Dickens asked, "Where is Mr. Barkis tonight?"

"Oh, he's out for skittles and beer tonight, with the carters. He used to be a carter before we came in here. He still does some driving on the side. I, myself, were in service. When me and Barkis wedded, we wanted to try and do something different. We got the inn on very generous terms, the good Lord knows."

Dickens said, "We'll drink to your success and good health. Happiness to both you and Mr. Barkis."

As we raised our glasses, (actually three glasses and one teacup) the door to the taproom opened another time. A finely dressed, slender woman entered and sat at a small table in the corner. A veil covered her face, and shadows in the corner hid any further details of her appearance. Immediately, Mrs. Barkis excused herself and hurried to the table. There she engaged in hushed conversation with the newcomer.

We four drank our beverages. The quiet conversation continued in the corner.

Finally, the mysterious lady rose and left. Mrs. Barkis maneuvered her bust and bottom toward the fireside. "When I was coming into the room, did I overhear someone say something about being in the business of recovering jewels?"

Chapter 2

Mrs. Barkis squeezed her fanny into a pine chair. She leaned toward the four of us to the extent her bosom would allow. “I have a wish to speak to you in a most confidential way.” Four male heads leaned into a huddle with the mistress of the Black Lion. “The fine lady that has just left this establishment needs help quite bad. There would be a grand reward for those what could help her.”

Mr. Dickens suggested, “Perhaps you could explain the problem to us, and our good friends, Blathers and Duff, can tell you if they will be able to be of assistance.”

“Ah, that I would like to do, but I need to know there will be no repeating what you hear, outside this here room. An important lady’s reputation is to be ruined if this tale was to appear in one of your books, Mr. Dickens.”

“You have my word, Mrs. Barkis. None of my characters are anything like real people.”

“I trust you, Mr. Dickens.”

“Well then, what’s the story?” Blathers asked.

“Oh, my lady has made a terrible mistake. I’m afraid she has had a ’signation with a rogue.”

“Indeed, what is a ’signation?” Forster said, again putting his finger by the side of his nose.

"You mean an assignation, do you not, Mrs. Barkis?" Dickens' use of language was his livelihood.

"What's an assignation?" Blathers asked.

"A tryst, a meeting between lovers. Isn't that what you mean, Mrs. Barkis?"

"Exactly, and that's the problem. He's dead, and the pearls are gone."

Chapter 3

"Please don't be thinking poorly about my lady. She's not the kind to be out and about with men all the time. I guess she must have fallen in love, but she won't say. All she'll say is she were alone with the man in a small house in Spitalfields. She were required to leave the house in a hurry and left her necklace behind."

Dickens said, "Don't worry, Mrs. Barkis. This is not an unusual case. Even though society imposes high moral standards on the love lives of respectable women, love must not be denied."

"Indeed." Mr. Forster glanced in Mr. Dickens' direction. "Let he who is without sin cast the first stone."

Dickens' face turned pink. "Now, John, no tales out of school, please." The writer's reputation with the ladies was rising as fast as his literary fame.

Blathers looked at me and raised his bushy eyebrows. I shrugged my shoulders. Blathers frowned. I nodded. Blathers' head moved up and down in agreement, and he spoke, "Mrs. Barkis, Mr. Duff and meself is thinkin' we may be able ta be o' service to your lady. Can ya arrange a meetin'?"

"I can, and I will. I do hope you and Mr. Duff are armed. I think there has already been a murder."

Chapter 4

The following day, about midmorning, Blathers and I returned to the Black Lion. Instead of seating us in the taproom, Clara Barkis ushered us into her private apartment at the rear of the inn. As soon as we were seated and served tea—no brandy was offered—a carriage eased its way down the back alley. The lady, dressed exactly as she had been the night before, entered through the rear door. Blathers and I rose to our feet. Clara introduced us. "This is Mr. Blathers and Mr. Duff, the private detectives I spoke of." She did not mention the lady's name.

"Gentlemen, please be seated. I sincerely appreciate your offer to help me. Quite frankly, I have nowhere else to turn, and I must rely on your discretion. I hope I can do that."

I spoke for the partnership this time. Blathers thought I had a better command of the language and would make a better impression on the upper-class client. "We wish to be frank with you too, madam. This will be our first case as private inquiry agents. As Mrs. Barkis might have told you, we were, up until a while ago, agents of the Bow Street Runners and the Metropolitan Police. Hence, as you are our first client, we are very anxious to please you to the utmost. You can count on our discretion, and we will hope we can count on you to mention our names to others, should the opportunity come up." I had spent most of the prior evening rehearsing.

"I think we understand each other." The lady lifted her veil.

Blathers and I each gasped with surprise. I said, "We are honored to be of service, madam."

The meeting proceeded. "I was with a man in a house. There was an attack, a loud banging, as with some sort of club, at the front door. My friend, the man, John, hurried me out the back, where a carriage waited. As I was obligated to make a hasty departure, I left my reticule behind. My pearl necklace was in that bag. When I was getting into my carriage, I heard a ruckus, loud shouts, and furniture breaking. Later, my husband told me about an unusual killing that day. When he told more about what had happened, I knew it occurred at the house I had visited." As the lady continued her story, I took notes, getting details of the when and where, but I didn't write down any names, except that of John, the murder victim. When necessary, I referred to our client as "The Lady." I carefully avoided her husband's name. Finally she said, "That is the whole story, gentlemen. You can appreciate my predicament. Please report to me through Peggotty. I mean Mrs. Barkis. Dear Clara. God's speed and be careful. John has been killed already." Tears came to her as she lowered the veil.

Chapter 5

As soon as the lady left, Blathers and I went to the taproom. He wanted a brandy. Mr. Dickens and Mr. Forster were enjoying cheese sandwiches and dark ale for their lunch. Each put down the newspaper he had been reading. Mr. Dickens said, "Gentlemen, tell us all about your meeting."

"Indeed, who is the lady, and what did she do that was naughty?" Mr. Forster sported a leering grin.

Blathers said, "You gents must know, our lips is sealed about any details o' our case. We wouldn't want folks ta say Blathers and Duff couldn't keep a secret, now would we. I'll just say some valuable jewels and a murder is involved."

Dickens said, "Ah, yes! I think I read about a murder in Spitalfields in *The Times.* That paper is full of news today. There was a fire at the Tower of London, and another streetwalker has been brutally slain."

"Well, you'd think the Metropolitan Police would be able ta catch the bloody rascal what's killin' them girls. If me and Duff were on it, we'd get him. I wonders if'n it's that young Squod."

"It may be. They found a Jack of Spades at the scene. I'm sure you wouldn't miss him a second time. But, you know, if it is Jack Squod, then he must be living around here somewhere."

I said, "We have not forgotten about Jack Squod, Mr. Dickens. While we have been busy trying to earn a living, it does vex us that the young murderer escaped. If we caught the rascal, we'd be famous."

"You are famous. You know, I used your names once already in one of my stories. I hope you are pleased to be presented as the honest, hard-working men you are."

"I hasn't yet had the pleasure of readin' your book, but I'm sure you did right by us. Duff, does ya know we is in one o' Mr. Dickens' books?"

I said, "I do, but I haven't read it yet either. I hope it is a great success, Mr. Dickens."

"Thank you, Mr. Duff. I hope the mention of you and your partner will help in your business as private investigators."

"Will you have some tea, Mr. Duff?" Mr. Forster asked.

"I would love a cup, but then it's time to be doing some investigating."

Dickens said, "I hope you are careful in your investigation. There are a lot of dangerous zealots about these days."

Forster assumed his usual thoughtful pose. "Indeed, the return of Sir Robert Peel as Prime Minister certainly has the Irish Catholics upset."

Dickens needed another pint. "Clara, where is the girl?"

"The Lord save us, Mr. Dickens. I've sent her home. We will be needing her tonight."

"Won't the lovely Jane be here, then?"

"I've just had a message from her. She won't be

with us for many months. She has to go to the North of England to care for an ailing aunt. We'll miss her."

Mr. Forster said, "Indeed, Charles will."

Chapter 6

Blathers and I no longer had the use of our gig. Sir Robert Peel confiscated it for his Metropolitan Police at Scotland Yard. Shoe leather was our source of transportation. The walk to the house we were seeking took about half an hour. The journey presented no difficulty to me, and Blathers needed the exercise.

The house was in the section of London known as Spitalfields, a neighborhood primarily inhabited by Jewish and Irish textile workers. The residents considered the police to be an annoyance. We were attacked there more than once when we were policemen. Now, the first order of business was to locate a certain character who was a leader among the ragtag population. It would be important to let the local people know we were not part of Sir Robert Peel's "Bobbies" anymore.

We knew where to look. The gin shops of the neighborhood, among the dirtiest and most disreputable in all of London, were the business and political centers of the community.

In the largest, noisiest, filthiest of all, a burly man with hairy arms came to meet us as we entered. "It's dem two rozzers now, isn't it. Duff, you're lookin' skinny as ever, special since it looks as Blathers has added to his belly. Why doesn't ya take dat skinny arse o' yars outa here afore yas gets conked, do ya see."

Blathers stepped forward and put his hand out in front of him. "Now, Conway, take it easy." Hugh Conway was the unofficial mayor of the Irish population of Spitalfields. His gin shop was the unofficial Irish town hall. "We is come to tell ya that we is no longer wi' the police. We is now private investigators, and the population o' the area has no longer a need to fear from us."

"Ya never gave n'one a break when ya was a rozzer. How do ya expect dat we can trust ya now, answer me dat?" Conway had been running this gin shop for as long as either Blathers or I could remember, but he never lost his brogue. "Fer two pence I'd toss ya in da slops in da street."

It was my turn. "Mr. Conway, our activities of the past were directed by a higher authority. We had no control at that time. If we were not always as fair as possible with the citizens of Spitalfields, it was because that is how we were told to act. Now, however, we work only for ourselves. This allows us to do favors for those who do favors for us." I raised my eyebrows. "If you get my meaning."

"Y'er sayin' as if'n I help ya dat when da time comes, y'll help me, is dat right?"

"Exactly, and we have business in the neighborhood. We only care about our task. We aren't interested in any other activities."

"Afore I'd be helping ya, I would know what your business might be, do ya see."

Blathers said, "We is investigatin' the killing what happened in the little house a few doors down the street."

"Ya mean da one where dat fella lived all alone. Ya know, dat's strange in dis neighborhood. Most places has one family all living in da same room, do ya see."

"Why do you think that was the case?" I asked "Why did he live alone when everyone else is crowded in?"

"'Cause, he could 'ford ta. Maybe he owned da property, or his da or some relative did. Ya never know 'bout dese tings."

"Can you tell us what kind of person he was?"

"He was da kind o' person dat don't go into no gin shops. Dat's all I know. His passing won't hurt me business one lick."

Blathers asked, "Was he Irish or Jew or what, do ya know?"

"I told ya all dat I know, now. If ya want me to tell da lads ta give ya a chance in da neighborhood, den I'll do so. But ya better be careful. Dere's some tough fellas round here dat's got dere own ideas. And ya better not be double-crossing me, or ya wont get out o' da neighborhood da next time ya come round."

I said, "Thank you, Mr. Conway. We will rely on you, and you can rely on us."

Conway got the last word. "Fer da sake o' your healt' I hope so. I'd hate ta see ya lying bleeding in da alley here, now." Conway raised his eyebrows and looked straight at me. "If'n ya get me meaning."

Chapter 7

Blathers and I left the gin shop without partaking of the beverages purveyed by the establishment. “Weren’t you thirsty?”

“I only takes me drinks in nice clean ’stablishments like the Black Lion.”

“It wasn’t so clean when Squod owned it.”

“I know, but Squod weren’t chargin’ fer the drinks. That lout Conway would make me pay.”

“The Black Lion is much cleaner now that Mr. and Mrs. Barkis own it.”

“It’s lovely, and I shall continue ta drink there as long as Mrs. Barkis ain’t chargin’, or them writer fellas is payin’.”

We walked toward the house that was the scene of the murder of the man that the lady had called John. *The Times* reported that the police had not yet identified the victim.

As we approached, I said, “Do you think the pearls are still in the house?”

“I doubts it, but we’ll have ta take a look.”

A Bobbie stood on guard outside the front entrance.

“Does ya know that lad, Duff?”

“I think it’s Young Cruncher. You remember his dad, Old Jerry, the resurrection man.”

Blathers said, “I do. Hello, Young Jerry Cruncher. Is that you in them shiny buttons?”

“’Tis me, Mr. Blathers. What’s ya doin’ ’ere in Spitalfields?”

I said, “We are just passing through. Do you remember me, Young Cruncher?”

“I does, Mr. Duff. Is ya two still partners, then?”

“We are. It seems neither of us can get by without the other, strange as that may be.”

“Ah, ya two was a legend at the Runners, wasn’t ya. It’s ’prisin’ ta all you didn’t join the Peelers.”

“We did for a while, but Sir Robert’s ideas and our ideas just didn’t mix.” It is, of course, a longer story than that, but Young Jerry needed a simple answer.

Jerry went on, “All me mates is sayin’ as ’ow the real ’prising thing is the two of ya is partners, at all. Ya don’t seem ta ’ave much in common, does ya.”

Blathers said, “We gets along, and that’s all ya and your mates needs ta know. Now, tell us why is ya standin’ in front o’ this here house, Young Jerry?”

“Ah, there’s been a murder ’ere, ’asn’t there. Me gov ’as told me ta stand ’ere and not let a’body enter, donch ya see.”

“Now that’s a shame, isn’t it, Duff? Here we is standin’ in front o’ a house where a murder has been committed, and we can’t go in. And us in the detective business and all. I bet if we had a wee peek we could see somethin’ that would help solve the murder.”

I caught Blathers’ wink and went along with the game. “Oh, yes, yes. And if we saw something that would solve the crime, we could tell Young Jerry here, and he could tell his gov and get promoted on the spot.”

“Think o’ it, Young Jerry, no more standin’ round

on the street, a big desk at the Yard, people thinkin' o' ya as a great detective. All for one wee peek, Jerry me boy."

Jerry's eyes widened, and a broad smile crossed his face. He must have been picturing himself as a famous detective. "I guesses, seein' as 'ow ya is detectives, it wouldn't 'urt for ya ta 'ave one quick look. But ya wouldn't tell me gov, would ya? I'd be in big trouble, donch ya see."

We hurried up the walkway before Jerry could change his mind, although there was little chance of that. The young constable had an odd look on his face, probably dreaming about his future as Sir Jerry, head of Scotland Yard.

The door was unlocked. Scotland Yard must have had great faith in their constables. I said, "Let's start with the bedroom. It's the most likely place the lady would have left them."

Blathers said, "And don't forget to look at everything with your mind's eye."

Blathers and I had learned a few things during our time as policemen. The techniques of searching a house, so no one would know we had done so, is one of them. We were methodical and careful, but doing a proper job required more time than Jerry thought of as a "wee peek," because he soon poked his head in the door. "I thinks ya should leave now. I takes it ya 'aven't found a clue ta solve this 'ere case."

"We are just about through, Jerry. We will only be about five more minutes," I said.

Blathers added, "Now don't you worry, Young Jerry. We'll never tell your governor about this at all. Just give us the time we needs. That's a good lad."

"But, donch ya see, if me gov comes along ta check on me and finds ya 'ere, I'll be back workin' wi' me da."

"You keep a good lookout there, Jerry lad, and if your gov is comin' 'long, just say, good 'n loud, 'Go'day, sir.' We'll be out the back door 'fore his foot hits the path."

Jerry was distraught. "Please, please 'urry, and gets out o' 'ere soon as ya can."

We carefully continued our search. Another fifteen minutes passed. Jerry paced up and down in front of the building like a little boy desperately in need of a bathroom.

Soon he came to the front door again, stepped in, and shut the door. "Please gets out o' 'ere right now, and use the back door. There's someone a lurkin' on the corner, donch ya see. It's not me gov, but I doesn't really knows who 'e is, and I doesn't like 'im watchin' me."

Blathers hurried to the front window and looked up to the corner. "Are we through here then, Duff?"

"We are."

"Then let's get outa here. There's a gent in a black greatcoat wi' the collar turned up watchin' this house."

"Sorry, Jerry, we didn't find anything, but don't worry. Nobody will ever know we were here, that is, if you don't mention it to anyone."

"Come on, Duff. Out this way. We'll make it up ta ya, Young Jerry."

Blathers and I scurried down the alley toward the corner where the stranger was stationed. When we got there, however, he was gone. He had walked to the house to talk to Constable Cruncher. Jerry was shaking his head vehemently and pointing down the street, as if to tell the stranger to be on his way. The stranger took something out of his pocket and held it out to Jerry. Jerry's head started shaking faster, and now he was stamping his feet, and he had his hand on his baton. The stranger shrugged and began walking back toward us. We ducked behind the buildings and watched. The stranger turned at the cross street.

When we were sure he was gone, we once again, accosted poor Jerry Cruncher. "Who were that man?" Blathers demanded.

"Oh, me, oh, my, I'm gonna get in big trouble o'er this job. I don't know who 'e were. Donch ya see, tha's why I chased 'im away. Now I'm gonna chase you two away, as well. I can't be seen talkin' to ever'body what comes down the street, now can I."

I said, "Now Jerry, we're not just anyone. You know us, and you should want to help us."

"Right," Blathers added. "Ya should want ta help us solve this here crime so as ta get some push wi' your gov. Besides, ya doesn't want ta make us angry. We might just not be as careful about talkin' about how ya already let us in the house."

Jerry took a deep breath. "A'right, a'right, but I doesn't know who 'e were. 'E sees ya go in, and 'e comes o'er ta find out who ya was. I told 'im ya was detectives from the Peelers, and was conductin' a routine 'vestigation, as I 'as been taught ta say. Then I chases 'im 'way right off, don't I. Now would ya please go 'way an' leave me 'lone, please, please."

"Okay, Young Jerry, we're goin', but we might has ta come back, ya see. How long does ya think ya will be standin' guard here then?"

“I ’opes not too much longer. I think they ’as collected all the bits and pieces what they needs, specially if you fellers ’asn’t found noffink. Donch ya see, there’s noffink more ta find.”

Blathers said, “That, Jerry me lad, ’pends upon where ya looks and what ya is lookin’ fer.”

Chapter 8

"All's we needs ta know is where is the damn pearls. We doesn't have ta solve no murder."

"Well, we might have to solve the murder to get the pearls back. Right now our best lead is the man watching us. Let's go back to the gin shop and ask about him."

"Okay, but we're not doin' no drinkin'. They says its drinkin' in places like that gives ya the typhoid."

I said, "It's all right to drink gin. It's the water that'll kill you."

"Well, I isn't drinkin' nothin' in that joint. We'll give Conway a tip fer any information we gets offa him."

The gin shop seemed to have achieved a higher level of filth just since we had been there earlier. As Blathers crossed the room, looking for Conway, I saw someone, apparently in a hurry to leave the establishment, bump him. "Get your hands off o' me wallet, or I'll break open your head, ya greasy mongrel, ya." He grabbed the pickpocket by the front of his shirt and jammed him onto a wooden bench. He pulled a cudgel from his coat pocket and waved it in the lad's face. "Sit right there and don't move, or I'll bang ya upside the head, and ya won't be pickin' no more pockets fer a long time."

I caught up with Blathers. “Who’s this then?”

“This be me friend the pickpocket. What’s your name, boy?”

“I ain’t gots no name.”

“No name, eh? Well, maybe you’ll be comin’ up wi’ one if’n I was ta hit ya on the ear.” Blathers waved the cudgel in the boy’s face again.

Hugh Conway noticed the commotion and was on the spot immediately. “What’s a goin’ on, now? Joe, I’ve told ya dat ya can’t carry on your business in here.”

Other patrons started to gather. “It’s them rozzers is gonna beat poor Joe.”

“They’s gonna get beat on themselves if’n they isn’t careful.”

Hugh said, “Now settle down, lads. Mr. Blathers here were just protectin’ his property, now, weren’t he. If’n Joe is a gonna ply his trade, he can’t do it here, now.”

I was facing the shop’s entrance during the fracas. I saw the door open. The stranger in the black coat looked in, saw what was going on, and turned back to the street. This gave me an idea. “Never mind, Hugh. Blathers and I are going to take young Joe the Dip outside. That’s your name from now on, lad. We’re going to make you part of our team. Come on, boy.”

“Now mister, ya ain’t gonna ’it me wi’ dat cudgel, is ya?”

Conway said, “Ah, Joe, you have gotta take it when ya’re caught. You’re just lucky dat dese gents ain’t wi’ da Runners no more or ya’d be spending da rest o’ your God-given life in Newgate.”

I grabbed the young man by the arm and started toward the door. The other patrons of the shop were starting to get ugly again, but I knew we had a little time to get away. No one had set down his tumbler of gin. "Let's go, Joe. We're not going to hurt you. We might need your help, and you might be able to make an honest bob or two."

Outside, the mysterious stranger was loitering across the street. I whispered to Joe, "Do you see that man across the street? He's just seen us." The stranger disappeared around the corner. "Here is what we want you to do, Joe. Hang around as though you are looking for a mark. Blathers and I are going to walk down the street and talk to that Constable down there. Do you see him?"

"I do. 'E's been dere fer a long time. Dere were a murder in dat 'ouse."

"That's why we're interested in the house, and we think the other man is interested too. When we go and talk to the Bobbie, I am sure he will come back around the corner and look to see what we are doing. That's when you go to work. We need to know where he lives. There's an honest sovereign in it for you if you can tail him and find that out. We'll meet you back at the gin shop later."

"Can yous do a l'il better dan a sovereign?"

Blathers said, "Now, ya scalawag, ya knows ya can pick pockets fer a week in this neighborhood an' ya won't make a sovereign. Just do us a good job here, an' there'll be more fer ya in the future. I likes a lad what has the guts ta try an' pick me pocket."

"I were just t'inkin' 'bout extra 'azzerd pay, ya knows, likes day gives ta da soldiers when day 'as danger. Dat guy looks as 'e might 'as a gun."

Chapter 9

We started off to return to the scene of the murder. “Should we try ta get inta the house again?” Blathers asked.

Down the street, Jerry Cruncher stood guard.

“I don’t think we’ll be able to confuse Jerry again. He just turned and looked the other way when he saw us coming.” I glanced back over my shoulder. “Ah, just as I thought, there is our stranger. Do a good job, Joe.”

As we approached the house, Blathers said, “Here we is ’gin, Young Jerry. I means, Constable Young Jerry. I means, Constable Young Cruncher. Still standin’ out in the weather, are ya? What does ya do if’n ya has ta pee, Jerry? Does ya have ta go now? If so, me and Duff will stand guard fer ya. Ya don’t want ta wet your pants fer your gov, now do ya?”

Jerry did look a little uncomfortable, so Blathers continued to suggest he needed a break. The more Blathers talked, the more Jerry hopped from one foot to the other. “Ya wouldn’t go into the ’ouse now if’n I was ta take a wee walk out back?” By this time, Jerry had stopped hopping, and was trying to cross his legs.

I said, “You can trust us, Jerry. I’ll stand right here, and I’ll hold on to Blathers if necessary.” Jerry set out around the building on the run.

“That wasn’t very nice.”

"I knows, but it did work, didn't it." Blathers started toward the house.

"Oh, no, you don't. I gave my word to Jerry. We may need him, so he has to trust at least one of us. Just wait until he gets back, and we'll go back up the street and set our mysterious friend on the run. He is our best lead."

Jerry returned to his post. "Young Jerry, me lad, go back round the buildin' and button up again. In your haste ya has all the buttons confused, and some o' your parts is showin'. Take your time, lad. Ya knows Duff is as good as his word. Now be careful. Ya doesn't want ta catch a chill in the privates."

Blathers' nonsense made me laugh, but we had business down the street. When I looked, the stranger was gone, and so was Joe.

Chapter 10

We decided to return to the Black Lion and report our activity to Mrs. Barkis. We also decided to eat while we were there. Blathers hoped it would be a free meal.

"I'm so happy to see you." Clara Barkis welcomed us with open arms. Given her size, both of us did our best to avoid the hug she seemed about to bestow. A handshake from Blathers and a couple of bobs of my head saved us from physical injury.

"Have you had your meal? How about some bangers and mash?" The words were music to Blathers' ears.

I said, "That would be lovely, Mrs. Barkis. Then if you'll sit with us for a spell, we'll tell you what we have found so far and ask you for some more information."

"Sally will bring the food in a jiff. Now, Mr. Duff, you'll take tea, as I recall, and Mr. Blathers, how does a pint of bitter sound?"

"It sounds like just the thing, thank ya, Clara."

Clara brought the beverages to the table, with a pint of bitter for herself. She then grabbed the one chair that seemed to be able to hold her and pulled it up close between us. "Now, me dears, have you found the jewels?"

Blathers supplied the disappointing news. “The pearls were not at the murder scene. But we does have another lead, and we’ll be findin’ out more this evenin’.”

I asked, “Mrs. Barkis, did the lady tell you anything more about the man, John? For example, he was living in a neighborhood where most of the people are either Irish or Jews. Did she say if John was either of these?”

“She did say he was not English, and, Lord save us, she wouldn’t say what his business was. He must have been mixed up in some of the shady dealings that seem to be going on in that part of the town.”

“Has she said how they has met up?” Blathers asked.

Clara told the story the lady had related to her. “It was at a fancy dress ball, it was. I’ve always said no good goes on at them affairs. When my lady attends one of these events, there is always a chamber set aside for her private use, in the case she needs to be alone for a moment. At this event she had not brought a maid with her, because the poor girl came down sick just when it was time to leave. When it became necessary, my lady went to her room alone. When she entered, she discovered him sitting there. I think he must have been in the wrong place by mistake. In any event, she said they just talked, but you know as well as I what kinds of things happen. He must have mesmerized her, for she’s always been very proper.

“When he left he gave her a paper with an address. A few days passed, and then—it must be she couldn’t help herself—she slipped away and went to the address. He was there, and, Lord save us, it must have happened again. That was when she lost the pearls."

"Why did she have the necklace with her?" I asked.

"It was a mistake, too. It was in the reticule she was carrying. She was to take it to be cleaned. Because she was in a hurry to leave home without being noticed, she grabbed the wrong bag. She put it on a table, Lord save us, next to the bed, and then forgot it. I think the poor woman was quite badly smitten, do you see."

Blathers took a turn. "I still doesn't see why this particular jewels is so 'portant to the lady."

"Her husband gave it to her. It has been in his family for centuries and is very different, and not able to be matched. All of his female ancestors have been painted wearing the necklace. He expects she will wear it, and she is due to sit for the painter next month. She has told him she has sent it to be cleaned, to gain some time, but soon he'll become suspicious. Will you have another pint, Mr. Blathers?"

"Ah, you're a fine, fine woman, Clara my dear. A bird can't fly with one wing, now can it."

Mrs. Barkis brought more ale and tea. She had another pint herself. "Barkis has himself a cartin' job today, so I'm in charge of the taps." Sally served the bangers and mash. The mistress of the Black Lion sipped from her pint and said, "You don't think that someone will break the necklace up to sell the jewels separate, do you? Lord, I hope not. It will be the end for my lady."

Chapter 11

"Me feet is startin' ta kill me. All this walkin'." Even though the day was cold and damp, perspiration was showing on Blathers' forehead. He struggled to keep up with my long stride. I am quite a bit taller and, I must say, very much thinner that he is. "Can we slows down just a wee bit, so as I can get me breath?"

"We're almost there now. Just around the next bend. You didn't need a second pint to wash down your bangers and mash, you know."

As we approached Conway's gin shop, I saw Joe the Dip hanging around on the corner. Blathers went over and put a hand on the boy's shoulder. "What does ya have ta tell us now, Joe?"

"Le' me see da sovereign."

Blathers tightened his grip. "Joe, we needs ta hear your story afore ya see any cash. Come on, out wi' it."

Joe had a bent spine and a twisted left leg, like many of the young people in Spitalfields. These deformities usually resulted from spending years in a textile factory, standing in front of a machine for thirteen hours a day at an early age. "Awr, your breakin' me back, now."

Blathers hauled Joe into an alley beside the gin shop. I followed and said, "Blathers, let the lad go. You're hurting him. Joe, tell what you know, and the sovereign is yours."

"I done likes ya said. I follered da gent ta 'is lodgin's. It's only in da next street, number 28, first floor front, least dats where da shade went down right arter 'e goes in da 'ouse. I 'angs round a bit and out 'e comes, but I ain't able ta foller 'im cause I 'as ta meets ya. Dat's all I knows."

I said, "Good lad. Here's your money. Now, you can earn another one if you'll watch the gent tomorrow and report back here. But be careful."

"T'anks much. I'll stick to 'im like dung ta me shoe." Joe limped off to follow his mark and his new, lawful, well-paying career as an assistant detective. It never occurred to him that he was following danger.

Chapter 12

The next day was like every day for the past fortnight. A cold fog blew up the river. Blathers and I met at a coffeehouse about half way between our separate lodgings. We both live on Thames Street. I have two rooms on the first floor rear, in a very nice house, overlooking the embankment near Blackfriars Bridge. Blathers lives in a ground-floor room, facing the street near Southwark Bridge.

"Me feet is killin' me this mornin'," Blathers complained. "It's a good show we has young Joe ta do some o' the legwork."

"As soon as we are done, we should walk back to Spitalfields and look in on young Joe. The only reason he is doing the following is the stranger would recognize you or me. If the stranger catches on to him, the boy could be in some trouble."

We finished our breakfast and, accompanied by much complaining on Blathers' part, headed off to see how our junior associate was doing. In Spitalfields we walked down the street where Joe said the stranger had rooms. In order to reduce the possibility the suspect might see us and become aware he was the object of surveillance, we hurried down the side of the street opposite the house. "I doesn't see no Joe," Blathers said.

"He must be off following the suspect, at least I hope so."

"I doesn't think so, for here he comes now."

"Joe?"

"No! The stranger."

"Keep walking, and don't let on we are doing anything but passing by. Is Joe anywhere in sight?"

"I doesn't see him anywheres. Either he's real good at follerin' or he's still in his bed."

"Or he has met some disaster."

"Good morning, sir." I nodded at the stranger as he passed in the street. "Well, at least that gives us a good look at him." The stranger was tall and muscular through the chest and shoulders, like a blacksmith. He was not wearing a hat. His light blond, almost white hair was parted in the middle and combed back on both sides. He gave me a confident smile as he acknowledged the greeting. He had happy-go-lucky gray-blue eyes and a mouth full of shining teeth.

"I don't think we was recognized," Blathers speculated. "What did ya make o' him?"

"I think he's Irish."

"As Irish as Paddy's pig." Blathers' people were originally from Ireland, and he knew what his countrymen looked like. "Then it's them Catholics as is mixed up in this."

"But aren't you Catholic yourself? I mean, you are Irish, you know."

"Me people were o' the Church o' Ireland, good Protestants. We had people what fought wi' Cromwell."

"Well, nonetheless. It's not only Catholics who want changes. Most of the Parliament supported the Emancipation Act."

"It's true, but there's a bunch o' them popish Irish still wants to fight wi' guns and bombs. It's them murderin' rogues what we needs ta fear."

I nodded agreement. Blathers looked around. "I still don't see Joe. It seems like he takes our money, and he's not a-doin' the job."

"I don't think he would do that. I'm worried."

"Maybe you is right there. He seems ta likes bein' a detective. I hope nothin' has happened ta him."

"We should go to the gin shop to see if he has been around there. We're dealing with some dangerous people. If Joe got caught spying on them, he might get hurt."

Chapter 13

We continued in the direction of the gin shop, and quickened our step as our apprehension about Joe increased. When we neared the end of the street, we passed the alley where we had made the deal with the pickpocket.

"Psst!"

"What did you say, Blathers?"

"Nothin'."

"Psst! 'Tis me. Joe. I'm watchin' me mark. 'E's just gone in ta dat 'ouse der. 'E passed ya right by. Did ya no see 'im?"

I said, "Oh, Joe, you're all right. Thank God."

"I'm just loverly. I 'as been up early and 'ad a loverly breakfast wi' part o' me money. I slept indoors last night. I ain't feeled so good in a long time. Now get on wi' ya so's da mark don't sees ya talkin' wi' me."

I smiled. "We'll see you later, Joe."

Joe winked and popped back into the alley. Blathers and I turned just as the suspect was coming back out of the house. He headed directly toward us. It was too late for us to duck out of sight. "Just stands where ya is, likes we is waitin' fer someone on this here corner," Blathers said. He stuck his hands in his pockets and tried to look casual. The stranger continued to walk in our direction. He had his right hand in the pocket of his coat, and it looked like he intended to confront us.

"Top o' the morning to ya, gents. I have seen you around the neighborhood on several occasions. Are you new residents of this area?" There was a definite brogue, but the man spoke with a cultured voice, and his choice of words indicated he was educated.

"We is just passin' through. We is waitin' fer a fella ta join us here."

"Ah, it must be that constable fellow I saw you talking with, yesterday. Well, you'll want ta be careful standing around here, now. This is a tough section of town. Sometimes ya need a constable just ta keep from being conked on the head. Well, good day, now." The stranger smiled: a knowing smile, a warning smile, a threatening smile? I wasn't sure of the meaning of the encounter, but I think both Blathers and I felt an increase in the chill in the air.

Chapter 14

"How is we fixed fer ready cash?" Blathers asked. I am in charge of the partnership finances, as I have had a bit of schooling in the practice of accounting.

"We still have quite a bit left from our work for the Vice Society, but we need to make it stretch, in case we fail to earn a reward in this case."

"Does we have enough ta get a cab back ta the Black Lion? I is feelin' the need fer a brandy. There's a real chill in me bones, and me feet is still killin' me."

I hailed a cab at the corner, and we rode in comfort to the inn, where Mrs. Clara Peggotty Barkis waited patiently for word of the pearl necklace. "Come in out of the cold and damp, and sit by the fire. Have ya found the jewels?"

"Not as yet, Mrs. Barkis," I reported. "But we still have grand hopes."

"I'm happy you stopped by, because I'm some confused by what I read in *The Times*. It says here the man killed in Spitalfields was named Benjamin Allen."

I said, "Didn't the lady say his name was John?"

Blathers said, "Clara, me dear, afore we gets into the case, can ya gets a little somethin' ta quell the chill?"

"Brandy and tea, as usual?"

"Brandy and tea it is, and thank ya very much."

Clara served the beverages. Of course, since Barkis, himself, was not on the premises, she included "a wee drop of brandy" for herself.

After the first taste was disposed of, she asked. "Well, gentlemen, where do we go from here? Do you have any explanation for John being called Benjamin?"

I answered, "This is the first we have heard of it. Do you still have the paper, Mrs. Barkis?"

"It's right here. It is just a short piece, you see." She handed the paper to Blathers, and he handed it to me.

"Why doesn't ya read it ta us, Duff."

I read the short news item: "The Metropolitan Police found one Mr. Benjamin Allen of Dublin, Ireland, dead in rooms that had been let to him in Spitalfields. He was shot in the back of the head at close range. The police suspect the death was an execution committed by some nefarious gang of criminals. The area is known to be headquarters for various criminal and anarchist groups."

"Oh! How could my lady ever have gotten mixed up in this sort of thing?"

I said, "Mrs. Barkis, I think we need to meet again with the lady. Why did she think that her lov-, I mean, her friend's name was John? You'd think at least he would use his right first name. The pearls are still missing, and if we are to get them back we need to have more information. Can you arrange a meeting for later today?"

"I'll send off a note right away. I'll try for a time around four. Will that be all right?"

"That will be fine, Mrs. Barkis. Now, Blathers, what say we try to run down Jerry Cruncher, and see if you can work your magic with him. I'll bet he can tell us a lot more about what the Peelers think about this case than the newspaper can."

"Ah, that young dumbbell. His father, Old Jerry, used to run messages in the City by day and rob graves by night. I'm s'prised Young Jerry didn't foller in the same business. I think he's in'erited his father's dumbness."

Chapter 15

Scotland Yard overflowed with activity. The old gig, which was our transportation when we were on the police force, was parked in a corner of the yard, not being used.

"There's a damn shame," Blathers said. "No one usin' that little gig, and me wi' me feet just a-murderin' me."

"Maybe, if we make some money off this case, we can come back and the Police will sell the gig to us."

"An' old Pincher must be part o' the deal. A gig is no good wi'out a horse."

"Right you are. Pincher is a fine horse. That fellow seems to be on guard. Let's ask him about Jerry."

The guard informed us it was Jerry's day off, and he was most likely to be found at The Blue Bear enjoying a pint or two with his dear old dad. "'Is dad's retired now. As Young Jerry has a steady job wi' the Peelers, he can 'ford ta buy the ol' man a pint now and then."

Blathers moaned, "Does this mean more walkin'?" He looked at the guard. "Is anyone usin' that there gig, I wonders?"

"Ya can't use that gig. That's reserved for personal use of the superintendent hisself. 'He loves that horse; Pincher is its name. And that brougham o'er there is the carriage of the Prime Minister."

I said, "Is Sir Robert on the premises at this time?"

"He is, but he only will stay a wee bit. He and some others is visitin' wi' the superintendent. Wait one second, and you'll see him come out."

Blathers nodded and said, "We might as well stand here a few minutes and see the man what's payin' our bill."

I just rolled my eyes. "Discretion is the art of princes and kings."

As Blathers was wondering what I was talking about, Sir Robert Peel, founder of the Metropolitan Police and recently made Prime Minister, appeared in the yard. He was a neat, hawkish-looking man. He appeared very set in his ways. For six years he had served as Chief Secretary of Ireland. His efforts to maintain the Protestant ascendancy during that period made him hated by Irish Catholics on a par with Cromwell himself. The great Duke of Wellington, called by all The Iron Duke, and a thin man in very expensive-looking attire accompanied him. They took turns shaking hands, smiling, and nodding to each other before they all three climbed into the waiting carriage and drove off.

****

At The Blue Bear, we found Jerry and his father sitting on a bench at a pine table near the fire. They each had both hands wrapped around a pint glass full of dark ale. Blathers spoke to the old man. "So this is your occupation now, Old Jerry?" On the street, people called them Old Jerry and Young Jerry. "Seems ta me I remembers a time when livin' weren't so elegant."

Old Jerry remembered us, particularly Blathers,

since he had interfered the most with the resurrection business. “Ain’t ya boys proud o’ me son ’ere? One o’ you’s own now, ain’t ’e.”

Blathers explained, “We ain’t wi’ the Peelers, ya knows, Old Jerry. We is in the private inquiry business, and that’s why we is here. We needs your fine, bright son here ta helps out wi’ a problem. You’d like ta helps us, eh, Young Jerry, ta shows your fine father what a bright boy ya is, wouldn’t ya now?”

Young Jerry seemed leery, but Blathers knew how to get the most out of him. “We’ll just sits down here wi’ ya now and gets ya another pint, and ya can show us all how smart ya is. Duff, I’m supposin’ ya wants tea, and ya gents is drinkin’ dark.” Blathers went to the service bar and ordered the drinks. “Mr. Duff, o’er there, will pays ya.”

When the serving girl had brought the drinks to the table, Blathers said, “Duff, why don’t ya explain our problem ta Young Jerry here, so’s he can show his da how smart he is.”

I said, “You see, it’s like this, Jerry. We had information the murder victim was named John. Now we read in the paper his name was Benjamin Allen, and we don’t know if he is the person we thought he was or not. You could help us out if you could tell us all you know about the victim. For example, did you see the body, and can you describe it?”

“I seen it, yes, and yes, I can describes it.” Old Jerry beamed with pride. Young Jerry, in an effort it impress his sire, continued. “’E were a wee, skinny littl’ feller from Dublin. ’E ’ad almost no ’air on ’is ’ead, ’cept a big brush o’ a ’stashe. On a runty little fella likes ’im it looked out o’ place, donch ya see.”

I said, “Do the Peelers have any suspects you know of, Jerry?”

“They ’as put the best men on the job. They is ’fraid of some Catholic plot.”

“Ah! Them Catholics, is it. I has told ya so, Duff.”

Jerry continued, “That’s just some o’ them. Others thinks it might be a bunch just gettin’ started what’s callin’ themselves soomthin’ ’bout charts.”

I said, “The Chartists. I’ve heard of them.”

“And there’s always them folks wants ta do soomthin’ ’bout the factories. There’s a lot o’ trouble out there.” Old Jerry, in support of his brilliant son, brought the wisdom of his maturity to the discussion.

“Then they don’t think it were just a robbery or somethin’ like that?” Blathers asked.

“Oh, no! Because the feller were an Irishman, that’s why they thinks there be some plot goin’ on, donch ya see.”

Blathers ordered another round. I declined another cup of tea and asked to be excused for a personal moment in the rear yard of the pub. When we all were settled again, Blathers said, “Young Jerry, ya has been of great help ta us.” Old Jerry beamed brighter. “We certainly hopes we can rely on ya in the future ta help us out likes ya has done here.”

Old Jerry made the commitment. “Yous can count on me boy anytime, I’m sure.” Young Jerry winced.

Chapter 16

The lady entered the Black Lion the same way she did before, quietly through the back door. Blathers and I, along with Clara, were waiting for her. When she saw there were no others present, she lifted her veil. “Good afternoon, dear Clara. Good afternoon, gentlemen. What news do you have?”

I said, “We are sorry to report we do not yet have the necklace. We are, though, making some progress. Unfortunately, information we have has confused us about who was murdered. We understood John was the name of the man you…er…met. Now we read in the news the victim’s name is Benjamin. Can you help us understand this?”

“The gentleman that I knew was called John. He may, however, have used other names under other circumstances. Have you a description of the victim?”

Blathers answered, “We does. He were a mousy little feller, wi’ no hair on his head, and wi’ a large mustache.”

“A moustache! John doesn’t fit that description at all. He was a well-built man, clean shaven, with a full head of light-colored hair that he parted in the middle.”

Chapter 17

We took a hack back to Spitalfields. We put out money for the cab because of a need to locate Joe quickly, not to preserve Blathers' soles. The driver dropped us at the gin shop. "If'n you're a-goin' ta dat joint, doesn't be 'spectin' me ta pick yas up." He wasn't of the highest class in England, but he wasn't low enough to go into that gin shop.

Blathers explained, "We is on official business here, now. We doesn't drink in a place like this."

"Sure, sure!" The driver shook his head and drove away.

"Never mind him," I said. "Let's start searching for Joe." The first place we looked was the gin shop. "Say, Conway, have you seen Joe the Dip around today?"

"He were by here just a bit ago. He says ta tell ya, if'n I sees ya, dat he's hot on the trail of somethin', and he'll meet ya here at six."

Blathers said, "We'll wait down the street."

"Me place ain't good 'nough fer the likes o' ya, now, is it?"

As usual, I covered for my partner. "We just need to take another look at the house down the street. We'll be back." We hurried out of the dank room before we were required to touch any of the filthy drinking vessels used to serve the regular patrons. We walked to the murder scene once again. No one was on guard now.

"Does we wants ta look inside again?" Blathers asked.

"It wouldn't hurt. The last time, we were looking for the necklace. I'm pretty sure it's not there, but we might find something we weren't looking for that'll help us."

We went to the back of the house. The door was locked. Blathers reached in the pocket of his greatcoat and removed a little box containing several small tools. Seconds later, the door popped open. Blathers has some unusual skills. I told him, "Nicely done. That's one of the reasons I've kept you as a partner."

"Ya has kept me 'cause ya can't get by wi'out me. The question is why has I kept ya."

Inside, Blathers started on the ground floor and I went up to the first floor. I heard Blathers searching the front room, so I yelled, "Blathers, come up here now. Hurry!"

I was on my knees on the floor of the front room. I held Joe in my arms. Blood dripped from a wound on the crippled lad's skull. "He's still alive. Quick! Go to the street and get a cab. We need to get him to a hospital, fast." Blathers ran down to the street. It was just beginning to get dark and foggy. I heard him call, "Cab, cab. Wait right here, I'll be right back. It's a 'mergency." When we got to the street, I saw it was the same driver who had dropped us at the gin shop earlier.

He shrugged and shook his head, but he waited while we got our injured friend into the hack. "The 'spital is right near, gov. We'll be there in a sec." The hack jolted forward.

****

Blathers and I, and the cabdriver, waited outside the hospital while Joe was being cared for. Finally there was word. "Sister, how is Joe. Will he live?"

"He'll be fine, but he needs a few days' rest. Do you know, is he registered with any parish? We should see he goes to the facility maintained by his parish."

I asked, "Can you keep him until the morning? We'll be back for him then."

"I'll care for him tonight, but you'd best be here early, afore the gov shows up, or there'll be a row."

"We'll be here by half-seven. Is that soon enough?"

"That'll be fine. I'll see you then, right here." The sister disappeared into the hospital.

I extended my hand. "Driver, thank you for your help in this matter. What is your name?"

"They calls me Barbary, gov."

Blathers said, "We wishes ta thank ya fer your help, then, Barbary."

I added. "We haven't much cash on us now, but if you'll meets us in the morning, and help us to get the lad home, we'll be sure to pay you then."

I gave Barbary the name of the coffeehouse where Blathers and I met most mornings. Barbary agreed to join us and help transport Joe. We both were concerned about the boy's recovery, and we were also anxious to learn why he was attacked.

Chapter 18

We took Joe to my rooms and put him to bed with a dose of laudanum. He needed rest before he talked about what caused the attack, and what hot lead he was following. He tossed and turned, and small amounts of blood stained the bedding. I stayed with him, but Blathers was unable to sit around and went out to visit some of the known criminals in the city. He was looking for someone who would be in a position to fence a valuable piece of jewelry. Even though the attack on Joe had put an onus on us to punish the perpetrator, Blathers focused on our primary goal, to recover the pearls.

The whole affair seemed centered on the Irish population of Spitalfields. So Blathers said he intended to visit an Irishman who was suspected of participating in less than legal transactions. The man had started as a smuggler and black marketeer during the Napoleonic Wars. Now, years later, he still had sufficient wealth to front sizable deals in hot jewelry. The police suspected he used some of his funds to stir up unrest among Irish nationalists. The rumors of an armed uprising in Ireland had become stronger with each passing year.

Those Irishmen who engaged in illegal businesses usually maintained premises in Spitalfields, where Irish immigrants elected to starve in England, as opposed to starving in their native land. I have heard stories, though, that the more well-to-do Irish businessmen, regardless of the legality of their enterprises, were often the first to provide help to their neighbors when it was needed. They kept as many alive as they could.

Blathers intended to call on Caddy Quale, the most renowned of the Irish "men of business." Caddy and Blathers had confronted each other many times when Blathers and I were Bow Street Runners. Blathers knew where to find him. To get there he had to go down an alley behind two rows of three-story buildings. At the third house on the right, a door sat exactly in the middle of the wall; at least, it was in the middle when the house was built. Over time, the building tilted slightly to one side, leaning against the house next door, and took the door with it.

Chapter 19

Joe came out of his stupor late in the afternoon. I was preparing some beef broth for him when Blathers knocked on the door. Ever cautious, I went to the door with a lead pipe in my hand and asked who was there. Blathers identified himself. I set aside the pipe and unbarred the door.

"Joe's just having something to eat. I think he'll get strength from his broth, and we'll be able to talk with him."

"As ya knows, I has been doin' a bit o' investigatin' meself. I'll tells ya about it while young Joe's a slurpin' his soup. Are ya up ta listenin' ta what I has found out, Joe?"

Joe nodded assent, some broth running down his chin. Blathers told of his conversation with Caddy Quale. From his description, it seems the encounter went something like this:

When Blathers knocked, a tall, thin man with muscular arms peeked out. The top of his head was a round bald circle, but he grew the hair down the back of his neck, so that it touched his shoulders. "And what is it ya may be wantin' with me, Mr. Blathers, may I ask?"

"Lets me in now, Caddy. I needs ta talk wi' ya about some pearls."

"Faith, are ya robbin' houses now that the Runners is no more? Well, we all need ta make a living."

"I is in the private investigatin' business now, Caddy, so's ya has nothin' ta fear from me. I ain't able ta arrest ya."

"A private investigator is it now. Well, I'm not going ta let ya investigate me privates, and that's a fact."

"Stop the nonsense now, Caddy. I is in needs o' your help. Will you let me in so's we can has a chat? Ya never knows when I might be in a position ta do you a favor, ya know."

"Faith, come in, man. I don't think I'll ever need a favor from ya, but I ain't got nothing ta hide, and I always liked ya when ya was a Runner, even though ya aren't a Catholic."

Quale took Blathers up a narrow, tilted stairway. At the top, the dingy world of Spitalfields disappeared into luxury. There were two rooms. The first was a sitting room, office, and study combined. Its major piece of furniture was a large rolltop desk placed on the front wall. Beside it, hanging one above the other, were three miniature paintings of pastoral scenes, probably of places in Ireland. There was a large comfortable chair with a small table beside it.

The most impressive feature of the room, however, was the wall of shelves filled with books. Blathers had no idea there were that many books in the world. He picked up one from the table next to the chair. "What's this here book called?"

"It's *Common Sense,* by Thomas Paine."

"That's what I has come ta talk wi' you about, common sense." It was a good opening, but, unfortunately, Blathers didn't have any idea what the book was about.

"Ah, well then, you're familiar with the thoughts of Mr. Paine. That's lovely. Why don't ya have a seat? We can discuss his ideas, and how they apply to the Irish question."

"I isn't here ta discuss no Irish question. I wants ta talk about the pearls question."

"And faith, what does Mr. Paine have ta do with pearls? Except o' course his pearls o' wisdom."

"Don't ya change the subject on me. I doesn't know nothin' about any Mr. Paine. I doesn't want ta talk about him. But I does want ta talk some common sense wi' ya, that's all."

Quale must have smiled. Even though Blathers was telling the story, he couldn't hide the fact that Caddy was toying with him. "Faith, ya had me confused for a bit there, but now I understand. What is it ya want to tell me about pearls? What pearls are we talking about? That's a good place ta start, man."

Blathers said as he sat in the easy chair, no doubt frustrated, "All right! Now be quiet, and just listen. Ya might not be so confused." He proceeded to tell Caddy about the job he and I had taken on, without revealing the identity of our client. "We is of the belief our client would be willin' ta pay a substantial reward, wi', as they says, no questions asked. But the necklace must be returned wi'out no damage ta it. We needs ta gets it back as it were, and we needs it soon."

"Blathers, you know me. I don't do things that are dishonest. Dishonest acts hurt people, and I try ta help people, not hurt them. Now, mind you, there is a difference between dishonest acts and illegal acts.

Illegal acts hurt governments, and governments hurt people. It might be illegal acts help people. Do ya get me, lad?"

"Never mind the dishonest and the illegal and all that stuff. I thinks ya is tryin' ta change the subject again. Does ya knows where the necklace is or don't ya?"

"I don't. And if any Irish took it, I would. Ya say the man killed was from Dublin. Faith now, that's interesting. Most of my contacts are in southern Ireland. I should have known about this fellow. I'll tell ya what. Let me check with some of me lads, and come and see me tomorrow. Oh, and bring your partner with ya. I'll enjoy talking with such a bright fellow."

Blathers finished his report. "Say, Duff, does ya have anythin' round here ta help wi' me dry throat? I'm a bit parched, wi' all this talkin'."

"I can give you a cup of tea."

"Ah, what good would that do? Never mind. Now, I think if Caddy Quale can get hold o' them pearls, we can buy 'em back and all will be over."

Joe perked up. "If da Irish 'as got it, then Caddy Quale 'll finds 'bout it. Noffink 'appens 'mongst da Irish dat 'e don't knows 'bout."

I said, "That's good news then. It certainly seems that some Irish are involved. Maybe we'll be able to get the necklace back to the lady soon and close this case. That is, unless we want to discover the murderer and find out who tried to do in Joe."

Blathers argued, "We doesn't has ta find no murderer. People is gettin' murdered in Spitalfields, Saint Giles's, and Seven Dials all the time. And them is the lucky ones. The rest is just slow starvin' ta death."

"What about the attack on Joe?"

"Now Joe, me lad, did ya see who it was has conked ya on the head?"

"I didn't. But I knows dat it wasn't me mark."

I asked, "How do you know that, Joe?"

"'Cause I seen 'im runs out'a da 'ouse afore I goes in."

"You went in the murder house after the stranger ran out. Why? Maybe you better start at the beginning." I was amazed by the boldness of the young pickpocket.

"First I tails 'im ta da Black Lion." Joe told how the stranger went into the pub and stayed for a few minutes. "When 'e comes out, 'e goes ta da 'ostler and 'e's talkin' wi' 'em a bit. Den 'e gives da 'ostler a paper o' some kind." Joe followed his mark to a coffeehouse, where the man had a meal. "'E takes a long time ta eats, like 'es waitin' fer somefink."

When the mark left the coffeehouse, he walked to Spitalfields. "Me feets 'urt much as me 'ead." Joe complained. Blathers lifted one foot and then the other, grimaced, and rubbed his head in approximately the same place where Joe was wounded.

In Spitalfields, Joe saw the stranger enter the murder house, but just as he got to the door he seemed to hear something, so he turned and ran. It looked like he was clutching some package under his shirt. Joe slipped into the house by a side window. Apparently picking pockets was not his only talent. When he got inside, he thought he heard a noise on the upper floor. He went to investigate, and as soon as he entered the front room, the lights went out.

After finishing his story, Joe speculated, "Dat feller is Irish, fer sure. But 'es not one o' dem dat's usually

’angin’ round da gin shops. ’E’s different den dem odders. Even different den Caddy Quale. But what I can’ts figure is why ’e’s went ta da Black Lion.”

Chapter 20

Barbary met Blathers and me for breakfast the next morning. He offered to have his cab available for us, as needed. I suspected Blathers had made some kind of deal with the driver. I had to admit (only to myself, of course) that having transportation readily available was a benefit.

Joe stayed in my rooms to rest for a few more days. I was thinking I might have enough room in my place that Joe could move in permanently. If it weren't for his experience in the textile factories, and the resultant crippling of his body, Joe probably would have led a quite different life. I was thinking about giving him a chance to become the type of person his intelligence and diligence indicated he could be.

Neither Blathers nor I had ever married. Blathers didn't seem to be the type to settle down and raise a family, and while I would like nothing better than a home-sweet-home situation, I find it difficult to talk to the type of woman who would be appropriate for the home I envision. Being a stepfather to Joe, however, might just be like having a family.

After breakfast, Barbary drove us to the Black Lion. It was still early enough that Clara was busy cleaning and preparing for the noon trade. Blathers accepted "a wee bit o' brandy," and Barbary and I had tea. Barbary, realizing our business with Mrs. Barkis was confidential, took his tea into the taproom, while we got our heads together in the parlor. The parlor was now vacant. The morning coach had just left.

Clara said, "Ah, there's fewer and fewer taking the coach, now them trains has started up. They do make some awful noise and soot. I hope they don't come too close to this place."

"The trains will bring great changes to London and all of England. Mark my words," I prophesied.

"We hasn't come here ta talk about trains, Clara," Blathers said. "What we needs ta know is about a feller what were here yesterday. Our lad, Joe, trailed him here, and he leaves a note wi' the hostler. Does ya know what that's about, does ya?"

Mrs. Barkis lowered her eyes and stared at the tabletop. "It was a note for my lady. I took it to her yesterday, after the midday meal was done. She said she wanted to meet you two again, but she can't get away for a few days. Instead she sent you this. She said we three should read it together." She handed a note to Blathers. He handed it to me.

I broke the seal and read:

Dearest Clara and Dear Gentlemen,

There has been a serious misunderstanding. The man who was found murdered in the house was not the man with whom I was acquainted. The man about whom I inquired, John, is still alive and has been in touch with me. He has my necklace and wishes to return it.

Unfortunately, it will be very dangerous for both of us if we meet. I therefore need your help in retrieving the jewelry.

I believe the best way to handle this would be for Mr. Blathers and Mr. Duff to meet with John and obtain the necklace from him. They then should bring it to dear Clara, and she can bring it to me without giving rise to suspicion on anyone's part.

John will be in the neighborhood of the gin shop in Spitalfields at about six in the afternoon for the next several days. I am told that you gentlemen will recognize him. He will have the necklace with him, and he will give it to you without further ado.

I wish to thank you gentlemen for your service. Clara has an envelope for you, which she will give to you when you hand her the necklace. I trust the contents will be sufficient to cover your fee and expenses."

The note was not signed.

I said, "Mrs. Barkis, we will bring the jewelry to you as soon as we get it. Will you be able to take it to the lady tonight?"

"I will, but I would be happy for your company at least part of the way. I am sure you have recognized the lady, so it won't be any problem if you see where I go. But you won't be able to come on the grounds, so if you'll just go with me as far as the gate, then the job will be done."

Blathers wasn't so sure. "Aye, it'll be done, if'n this here John ain't a dangerous murderer, or if'n the ones what did kill the lad from Dublin ain't lingerin' around the gin shop. I'd best bring me pistol fer the evenin's activity."

Chapter 21

Barbary dropped us each at our own lodgings. He promised to pick us up again later in the afternoon for a trip to Spitalfields. Blathers intended to look for his gun and soak his feet. They still ached from all his walking before Barbary came along.

I planned to spend some time with Joe and perhaps talk to him about moving in. I knew stories about young lads who, having either been born into poverty or later achieved that state through the folly of their parents, had been rescued and developed into persons of renown. There was a rumor that Mr. Dickens had suffered as a child and been forced to work in a factory for long hours. I was sure there was a school in the neighborhood that, after he'd had some basic instruction by me, would accept Joe, even though he might be a bit older that the usual student. I also needed to find out Joe's last name. After all, I couldn't enroll him in a school as Joe the Dip.

I opened the door quietly. "Joe, Joe, are you asleep?" No answer. "Joe, it's just me. Are you here?" No answer. I looked in his bedroom. No Joe. Louder now, "Joe, Joe, where are you?" He wasn't there.

I couldn't guess where he would have gone. Did he leave a note? Of course not. He couldn't write. Perhaps he'd spoken to a neighbor. I knocked on the door of the tenant downstairs. There was no answer. I banged louder. Still no answer. I ran out to the street. A costermonger was selling fruits and vegetables. "No, I 'asen't seen noffink, gov."

A Bobbie stood on the corner. "Have you seen a crippled fellow? Maybe you know him. His name is Joe. He used to be a pickpocket."

"'Ow would I see a pickpocket? Them's the kind what 'ides from me."

What to do? Where to go? Joe is missing!

I started toward Blathers' rooms. *Maybe Joe went there looking for us.* I asked along the way. No one saw "noffink." I came across another Bobbie. *The Metropolitan Police are as blind as the thieving street peddlers.* At Blathers' lodgings, nothing. Blathers was taking a nap. He hadn't seen or heard from Joe.

"Waits just a bit till I gets me gun. We'll try ta find Barbary and gets a ride ta the gin shop. Maybe Joe decided ta go home. I thinks the gin shop is the closest thing he has fer home."

I waited. Blathers put his pistol in the pocket of his greatcoat. He took forever. We headed into the street. At the first intersection we found Barbary. I told him, "Joe has gone missing. Can you take us to Spitalfields right now?"

"'Op in!" Barbary snapped his whip, and we were off.

Chapter 22

Blathers went into the gin shop to ask if Hugh Conway had seen Joe. He hadn't.

I went down the street to the house that was the scene of the original murder. Could Joe have gone back for a second look at the place where he received his first injury? The front door was unlocked. Joe was there in the front room. Additional blows to the lad's head had finished the job started the day before. He was dead at my feet.

When Blathers entered the building, he found me slumped to the floor, wiping my eyes. Blathers yelled out through the door, "Barbary, get them Peelers. There's been another murder in this here house." He reached out and put his hand on my arm. "I'm sorry, Duff. I knows how ya felt about the lad. Come now. We has some jewelry and a bastard murderer ta find."

Chapter 23

At the Black Lion, Blathers was having a brandy, compliments of Clara Barkis. I also had a glass of brandy in front of me. "Go ahead and drink it, Mr. Duff. It'll help with the pain. I know how attached you were to Joe. He's with his maker now, and all his aches and pains are over."

I know Blathers understood how I felt, but as usual, he focused on the business at hand. "We is sorry we isn't able ta deliver the jewelry, but the feller never showed up. O' course, there were so many Bobbies around he were probably scared off."

The door opened and Charles Dickens and John Forster strode in. "Good evening, Mrs. Barkis, and good evening to my two favorite detectives. Barkis, himself, is off again this evening, I presume." Dickens noticed Clara had her hands wrapped around a pint mug.

"He is. He has a hauling job tonight. He just can't seem to get away from that calling and settle down as an innkeeper. That leaves a lot of work for me, but then again, the carting pays well, and it's all money, I always say."

Forster said, "Indeed, I think he was born a carter and will always be a carter."

Dickens said, "That may well be true, but then

carting is an honorable profession, as is inn-keeping, Mrs. Barkis. Of course, Forster and I prefer an innkeeper who will see we are provided with a couple of brandies."

"Coming right up, Mr. Dickens."

"Now, Mr. Duff, your face is longer than usual this evening. What's the difficulty?"

Blathers explained about Joe's death, and my plans to help him. Dickens offered his condolences and added, "It's very laudable of you to care about someone in such circumstances. Most of our society turns away from the plight of the poor, which has been occasioned by the development of industry in our fair nation. It is difficult to understand how some can ignore the suffering of their fellow man."

Forster put his index finger along the side of his nose and said, "There is more to it than that. It is a dangerous society where the rich get richer and the poor get poorer. Indeed, witness what happened in France."

I said, "Some are saying that Sir Robert only founded his Metropolitan Police force to protect the rich from the poor. They say, if the French had Bobbies, there wouldn't have been a revolution."

Blathers expressed his opinion. "Them Bobbies isn't much good at nothin'. There has been two murders in that house now, and nobody knows a thin' about either one o' them."

Dickens agreed. "Look at the number of young women slain in the streets each year. The police seem helpless in those cases."

"They needs ta nab that young Squod. He's probably the one what's doin' it. I is sure he is around here somewhere. If'n they'd put out a good reward for the rascal, Duff and me would get him."

While this conversation was going on, the hostler came to the door and signaled to Clara. She set the drinks for Dickens and Forster on the table and went to him. He handed her a folded piece of paper. She read it and looked over at the benches near the fire. "Mr. Blathers and Mr. Duff, could I speak with you in the parlor for a moment? Mr. Dickens, Mr. Forster, we'll only be a short time."

Chapter 24

"I have another note from that fellow John. He wasn't able to meet you because, as he says, some dangerous people were following him. He's not sure who they are or what they plan to do. He still has the necklace and suspects they want it, but he doesn't know why. He also thinks they are the gang that killed poor Joe."

I began to pay attention to what was happening for the first time since the discovery of Joe's body. "I'll get them if I die trying." That was all I said.

Blathers said, "Clara dear, I knows it's our job ta gets the jewels back, but now we also needs ta get the rats what done in poor Joe. I thinks Duff agrees that they is both the same job. If we catches the killer, we'll get the jewels."

Clara said, "I agree, and I'm sure my lady will also agree. Seeing as how young Joe died trying to help find her necklace, she'll be happy to support both efforts."

We rejoined the men of literature in the taproom. "Gentlemen, thank you for your patience and understanding. I know that, as a writer, Mr. Dickens, you have a natural curiosity about things, but this, as you also know, is a very delicate affair."

Dickens responded, "My dear Mrs. Barkis, my good friend Forster and I have already pledged our silence regarding this matter. We now reaffirm that pledge, don't we, John?"

"Indeed we do, Charles. It is never our intent to prosper based on the misfortunes of others."

Blathers put his index finger to the side of his face and said, "Indeed, me and Duff makes our livin' 'cause o' the misfortune o' others."

At that point another customer entered the taproom. He sat at a small table at the opposite end of the room from us. Clara rose to attend to his needs. After providing him with a pint of bitter, she returned to the table. "Mr. Blathers and Mr. Duff, I'm going to start charging you rent. Folks are thinking this is your office. The gentleman asked me to tell you that Sir Robert Peel is waiting in a carriage outside, and he wants to talk with you."

I came to life for a second time. Blathers put his index finger along the side of his face for a second time. "Indeed."

Chapter 25

The brougham was parked in the yard at the side of the inn. All four horses stood quietly in the fog, waiting for a command from the driver. As Blathers and I approached the carriage, the door opened. "Step in, gentlemen. I believe there is room for you on the opposite seat. I think you are acquainted with Constable Cruncher." Young Jerry sat across from us, next to the formidable Sir Robert Peel.

"Good evenin', Your Lordship. Good evenin', Young Jerry." Blathers' fanny slid across the seat, leaving room for me. I remained silent.

Sir Robert said, "Gentlemen, Constable Cruncher tells me you have taken an interest in a certain house in Spitalfields where two murders have been committed."

I became alert, and raised my head from the downcast position that had been its posture for most of the night. I glared at Sir Robert. I jabbed my index finger toward the worthy. "We are more interested in the second murder. The fellow was an associate and special friend of ours. We want vengeance for his death."

"Please, Mr. Duff, calm yourself. I too am very interested in getting to the bottom of these crimes. Many of my colleagues are fearful of another Guy Fawkes type of plot. The Duke of Wellington is concerned there could be riots similar to the French uprising of the last century. Now that the Emancipation Act has been passed, there is fear the papists will become emboldened and attempt to overthrow the established church. Will the monarchy be next? We wish to forestall such activity before it grows like the labor movement has. But the government cannot afford another Peterloo."

"What has this all ta do wi' us?" Blathers asked.

"It is my understanding you are acting on behalf of a client, attempting to locate a certain gentleman known as John."

I expressed surprise. "How did you come by this information?"

Blathers added angrily, "'Has ya been havin' us follered?"

"Gentlemen, if you please, I respect that you owe a duty of confidentiality to your client and your sources. I too must remain confidential regarding my methods. Let me just say that I am not always as unaware about what is happening around me as it may seem."

I said, "So you know something about our activities. Why did you want to talk to us? Is this a warning?"

"Quite the contrary. I would like to work with you to help solve these murders and discover if there is a plot against the monarchy." Blathers started to rise from the seat. "Now, now, don't get excited. I won't ask about your client or inquire about her, er, or his, problem. If I ask about something confidential, just say so, and I won't pursue it any further."

Blathers asked, "Does the Peelers still has that horse Pincher hooked ta that little gig?"

"They do."

"Would ya consider helpin' ta get that fer me and Duff, if we was ta help ya?"

"I think I could, provided you give me the kind of help I require."

"Here's whats we'll do. Let us think about the matter till tomorrow, and we'll come and sees ya in the morning."

"That is fine. At the office of the Superintendent, at Scotland Yard, about ten."

"Ten it is, then. So long, Young Cruncher. I 'most forgot you was there."

Chapter 26

"But we can gets the gig and Pincher if we goes along wi' the man. And, don't forget, he's a very powerful man. We wants him on our side, we does."

"No, no!" I was adamant. "We are already committed to the lady. It would be a giant breach of our obligation to her to have anything to do with Sir Robert, and you know it. We'll have to do without Pincher and the gig."

"Ah, the devil! He already knows about the necklace, if'n ya was ta ask me."

"I think he is just bluffing. The only thing he knows is that we frequent the Black Lion, and his wife is close to Clara. He has put two and two together, but he's not sure about his answer. He's trying to trick us the same way you trick Jerry Cruncher. I, for one, won't fall for it."

"Maybe ya is right. Well, too bad, Pincher. How should we handle the meetin' tomorrow?"

"I'll write a note to Sir Robert explaining that, at second thought, we feel it would be a breach of our obligation to our client to work with him at this time."

Blathers took a big swig from his pint. "Okay, could ya says we would like ta talk ta him about Pincher after this be over?"

"We'll deal with that later. Right now let's

concentrate on the problem of retrieving the necklace and collaring Joe's murderer."

The Black Lion was not busy. Barkis, himself, was at home, so Clara was not holding court in the taproom, as she did when he was "off carting." Dickens and Forster were attending the performance of their play in Drury Lane.

Blathers and I finished our beverages and, since the usual stimulating conversation was not available, waved good night to Clara and stepped out into the dark and foggy street.

As the tavern door closed behind us, a link-boy, sporting a bright lantern, approached us. "Right dis way, now, gents."

"Naw, be off wi' ya. We doesn't needs no light, now."

"Ya is detectives, ain't ya?"

I answered, "That's right, lad. How did you know?"

"A gent gimme a penny ta fetch ya. If ya come wi' me, 'e's gonna gimme 'nother."

Blathers said, "How does everyone know where we is?"

I shrugged and said, "Who is this gent, then, boy?"

"'E says ta say 'is name be John."

"Lead on, boy."

Chapter 27

The link-boy led us down the street and around a corner. There, another carriage waited. It wasn't as grand as Sir Robert's equipage, but it was large enough to accommodate the both of us.

There was no one else in the vehicle. "'Ang on, gents." The driver threw a coin to the link-boy, shouted as he cracked the whip, and the cab leapt forward. The boy ran after the hackney coach. "Dis is only a ha'penny. Ya cheat!" The carriage rolled on.

Blather shouted up, "Where is ya takin' us, now?"

"'Tain't fer. Sit tight."

Soon the coach pulled into the yard of a small inn on the outskirts of London, almost in the country. A small church and graveyard were the nearest neighbors. "Ya'll finds 'im inside," the driver told them. "Me fare 'as been paid, but I is always 'appy fer a wee bit o' a tip."

Blathers said, "Don't take any wooden guineas. That's a tip fer ya, ya swindler, ya."

"I 'ope ya finds a'other ride 'ome."

"We'll gets home a'right. Now be off wi' ya. Ya'd cheat yer own mother fer a ha'penny, like ya did that poor lad."

The whip cracked. The cab lurched forward. We went into the inn. Blathers mumbled, "I guesses not all's them drivers is good as Barbary."

"Evenin', gents." The landlord approached us as we entered the taproom.

Blathers was still in a bit of a huff. "We's been kidnapped by a knave o' a hackney driver. Is there a feller here name o' John? He's the one what's sent the thief atter us."

"I am called John." A tall shadow rose from a secluded table in the corner of the room, away from the fire. Noticing our hesitation, he held a candle up so we could see his face. "Please come and be seated." There was no mistaking his brogue. Blathers and I each pulled a chair up to the table and sat down. Blathers felt in his coat pocket for his pistol.

"In my own country I am known as Sean, but in England, my mission is better served if I use the anglicized version, John."

Blathers was still a little hot. "Why has ya kidnapped us this way? I don't like bein' forced ta do nothin'."

"I am sorry. Please accept my apology. I have been trying to meet with you for two days, but enemies have made it difficult. I wish to have the necklace returned to the lady, but they want it to expose me and, at the same time, take revenge on Sir Robert."

I asked, "Do you have the necklace with you?"

"It is in a safe place nearby. The people who own this tavern are friends of mine. They have hidden it in a place where it can be retrieved readily but would never be found by those who wish to harm me and Lady Peel."

"What do you mean, take revenge on Sir Robert? Why is it you have enemies?"

“Right, who is ya, anyway? And how does we knows we can trust ya? A gent what has been havin’ a, I guess you’d say, a relationship wi’ a lady. I’d calls it somethin’ else, I would.”

“Perhaps I had best correct a misconception. If I can trust you, I will tell you all about myself, and about my relationship with the lady.”

I said, “Some explanation would help. We have already pledged to the lady that we will keep all we know confidential. I think we can make the same pledge to you, can’t we, Blathers?”

“As long as it don’t turn out ya done the killin’s.”

“I didn’t do any killing, and you will soon see that you can trust me. You see, I am a Catholic priest.”

Chapter 28

Neither Blathers nor I had ever seen a Catholic priest. We weren't absolutely sure what one should look like. We did, however, think he should be wearing some type of robe, or his clothing should be black and neat and new.

This person was wearing a gray tweed jacket. It was worn at the elbows, and frayed at the cuffs. He had brown corduroy breeches, like working men wore. The bottoms were quite soiled from dragging in the filth that filled the streets.

He definitely did not look like a priest.

Blathers felt for the gun in his coat pocket. "Do ya think we was born yesterday? We knows what a priest is supposed ta look like. We has priests in the Church of England, ya know. They doesn't look anything as shabby as ya."

"I know. This is a disguise. Even though the Emancipation Act has passed, Catholics are still not very welcome in London. In addition, my task is more delicate, and anonymity is required. You see, the lady is studying to become a Catholic."

"My goodness, why would she do that?" I asked.

"When she and Sir Robert lived in Ireland, she became friends with a Catholic family, the Fitzgeralds. That friendship has grown into a desire to convert. The

Fitzgeralds asked me to help the lady fulfill her wish. Unfortunately, the English still, shall we say, lack some respect for the Irish. So as to keep the conversion a secret, and to avoid persecution as much as possible, I have disguised myself."

I said, "So then, who are these enemies you are talking about?"

"I'm not sure exactly. As you know, there was a great deal of opposition to the Emancipation Act. The Iron Duke and Sir Robert only relented because of the fear of insurrection. They have made political enemies as a result of their change in position on the matter. I don't think even they know exactly who their enemies are, but it seems they are people who will go to extremes to get the Act repealed."

I understood. "So you think they are trying to get the necklace as evidence against the lady to embarrass Sir Robert?"

"I can see the story unfold in the newspapers right now, day after day: 'Lady Peel's Missing Necklace Restored'—'Who Is Lady Peel's Strange Male Friend?'—'Lady Peel Suspected in Love Affair'—'Worse—She's a Catholic.' Sir Robert's political career will wash down the Thames, and the duke's will follow."

The ever practical Blathers asked, "Well, where does we go from here?"

John answered, "It is important that we restore the necklace to my lady as soon, and as quietly, as possible. If our enemies get their hands on it, the game is over."

I said, "We can get it to her now. Just give it to us, and we will get Mrs. Barkis to help us deliver it."

Blathers objected. "Now, looky here. That rogue of a driver what dropped us off here can't be trusted. If'n we walks outta here wi' the necklace, we is most likely ta get jumped and robbed. We needs a plan."

Chapter 29

We discussed the plan with John for another hour. Blathers had brandy. I had tea. John had stout. I paid for the drinks.

The fog had thickened. We left the inn. Blathers and I walked toward the crossroad, hoping to find a cab. Blathers was closest to the wall that surrounded the church. I was on the left, the street side. Our shoulders touched in the darkness. As we passed an opening in the wall, an arm reached out from behind and circled Blathers' throat. He turned and ducked, thrusting his hip in my direction. I bounced out into the road. A cudgel aimed at my head grazed my arm. Blathers struggled with his attacker. I kicked the man. His grip on Blathers' neck slipped. Blathers reached in his pocket for his gun. I saw a fist strike him between the shoulder blades. The gun went off. There was a yelp. A shadow went dragging off into the fog. We could see three or four more shadows approaching. Blathers tried to pull the pistol from his greatcoat pocket, but it appeared to be tangled in the shreds left by the first shot. We now stood back to back awaiting the attack from what seemed like a large gang of ruffians.

Blathers struggled with his gun. Cudgels and chains were waving in the air. Blathers finally freed his weapon and fired a shot in the direction of the gang.

There was another cry of pain. Another shadow disappeared. The assailants retreated. A coach came charging down the street and stopped suddenly. Barbary yelled, “Blathers and Duff, get in. Quick!”

Blathers and I clambered aboard. Barbary cracked the whip. The gang gave chase, to no avail.

“Where in the devil did you come from?” I was able to utter the question that was on the lips of both of us.

Chapter 30

As soon as we were safely away from the attackers, Barbary slowed to a more reasonable speed. In the dense fog, we had been lucky not to have been in a collision. Blathers yelled up to the driver again, “How did ya happen along?”

Barbary yelled back, “Soon as we gets ta the Black Lion, you’ll see.”

Within a few minutes, the cab pulled into the yard of the inn. Barbary spoke to the hostler, “Feed dese fine young animals, and puts dem ta bed. Dey has done good work tonight, and deserves a rest. Come on, gents. We needs somethin’ ta warm our insides.”

The taproom was almost empty. The fog had sent everyone home early. The only occupants were Clara, squeezed with some discomfort into a chair in front of the fire, and Barkis, himself. Barkis was a wee man in comparison to his mate. He sat in a chair just like the one the hefty Clara occupied, but his feet barely touched the ground when he sat all the way back. There was also one customer—Caddy Quale, the Irish gangster or, perhaps, Irish benefactor.

“Faith, Blathers and Duff, you’re alive and well. Ya did good work, Barbary.”

“It were touch an’ go fer a time, dere.” Barbary seemed to know Quale well. “Ya wants ta know how I happened ta be on the scene o' your battle? Well, I works fer Caddy, and he asked me ta keep an eye on ya. When dat link-boy put ya in dat coach, I thought I best follow."

I said, "It's a good thing you did, or there would be pieces of me and Blathers all over the place."

Blathers added, "There'd also be some more fellers wi' holes in them. I wish I had left a few more bullets wi' them. Anyway, many a thanks fer rescuing us, but I doesn't understands how ya and Caddy is mixed up in this."

Caddy explained, "Ya met with Father Sean—I mean Father John—didn't ya, now. And he told ya about his relationship with the lady. Faith, doesn't he also serves as priest for many of the people I look out for. I pretty much support him while he's here. Sure, he's me brother. Not all me da's boys turned out ta be criminals, although some o' the English think as all Irish are, specially the priests. Me and me brother, together, we do our best ta make life for the Irish, them as have come here ta avoid starvin', more livable."

Duff asked, "If you and your brother are helping the lady, why did she get us involved?"

"Faith now, the problem is politics, ya know. There's someone trying ta get Sir Robert. If'n his wife was having a love affair it would be bad, but, because of his support fer the Emancipation Act, if'n it became known she was wanting ta be a Catholic, it would be worse. But the very worst news would be that she was acquainted with the Irish gangster Caddy Quale. I must stay out of it, and Father John dare not go near her or her house. We need the story ta be that you two recovered the jewelry from a person or persons unknown, not from Father John or with da help o' Caddy Quale."

Blathers said, "We is willin' ta helps all we can." He no sooner finished speaking than the front door of the inn flew open and a group of uniformed police rushed in. One, with a paper in his hand, stepped forward. "Is ya Caddy Quale?"

"Saints preserve us, I am."

"Well, we has a warrant fer your arrest, signed by the Queen's Minister o' Public Safety, Sir Percy Wesley. Ya'r accused o' planning ta cause a riot among the Irish. Ya'r ta come wi' us now." Caddy rose from his chair, and the remaining Bobbies rushed forward and surrounded him. They pulled his arms behind him and tied his wrists. Two of them strapped irons, connected by a chain, to his legs.

Chapter 31

Blathers and I weren't sure if any of the Bobbies recognized us. One or two of the older ones had been associated with the Runners and should have known us. Nevertheless, no one gave any indication they did.

When the Peeler in charge first mentioned Caddy's name, Barbary, who was still standing near the fireplace, turned and looked in another direction, as though he was not part of the gathering. Barkis hopped from his chair and began to busy himself by clearing empty mugs from the table.

Clara tried to jump to her feet, but she was wedged in the chair so tightly it took her several twists and turns to get up. She looked back at the chair as if to blame it for being too small.

Blathers and I both started to intercede in the arrest, but a look from Barbary cautioned us to remain uninvolved. We looked away in the same direction as the cab driver.

Clara said to the police, "We didn't know he was a revolutionary. We don't like that kind in here. Get him out, quick."

Caddy Quale went peaceably.

Chapter 32

The door closed on the backs of London's finest, and Barbary winked at Clara. "That were close. It's a good show only Caddy's name were on the paper, or we all could be in Newgate now."

"Isn't that the truth," Clara said.

Blathers looked at Barbary, Clara, and Barkis, himself. "What's a-goin' on here, then? Is there a kind o' conspiracy a-goin' on?"

Barbary said, "Sit down, now, and we'll tell ya all 'bout it. Dere's a conspiracy, all right, but we isn't da conspirators. Clara, tell da gents 'bout it."

Clara settled, and settled some more, finally fitting herself into the chair again. "You see, when Sir Robert Peel and the Duke of Wellington changed their minds and decided to support Catholic Emancipation, they made some powerful enemies. There are some that see this as an opportunity to gain power for themselves. They are conspiring to discredit Sir Robert and replace him with folks as would repeal the Emancipation Act. All that we're doin' is tryin' ta keep that conspiracy from succeeding."

I asked, "Who are the conspirators?"

Barbary said, "We isn't at all sure 'bout dat, but 'cause o' da arrest, it looks like one must be da Duke's cousin, Sir Percy. He signed da warrant."

Blathers said, "But a person like that don't dirty his hands wi' murder or fightin' in the streets. He must have some fellers doin' his dirty work."

"Right ya are," Barbary agreed. "If'n we can find out who da men on da street are, we can trace dem back ta old cousin Percy, and gets him tossed out on 'is backside."

I said, "The problem is fear. If people are afraid, they will do anything they're told."

"I fear dere's ta be 'nother arrest." Barbary said. "I 'opes it arn't Father John."

Chapter 33

Because of the arrest of Caddy Quale, and the potential for further action by the Queen's Minister of Public Safety, Blathers and I knew we had to act quickly to implement the plan worked out with Father John.

"But I hasn't ever been ta a Catholic Mass a'fore," Blathers complained. "I doesn't knows how ta act. They say them Catholics jumps up and down a lot. How will I knows when ta jump up?"

"Don't worry, just do what the person in front of you does."

"Well, truth be known, it isn't so much it be a Catholic Church. It's I hasn't been ta a church at all since I were a wee lad."

"Well, we're going now. Just think of it as part of the job. Come on, now. Barbary is waiting."

****

Father John saw us sitting in the back of the room. The "church" was merely the rear two rooms on the ground floor in the house in Spitalfields, the same house Joe had seen John enter and leave on his first day as a detective. Two rooms had been made into one by removing a wall. A table which served as an altar was at one end of the larger space. There was an additional small room to the side, where the priest put on his holy clothes, the vestry, I think they called it.

Father John gave a short sermon. His topic was about having tolerance for all mankind, even the Tories. After the sermon he announced, "There has been a change in my schedule. I will be unable to hear confessions this afternoon. For those in dire need of confession, I will hear them immediately after Mass. In order to insure privacy, I will hear confessions in the vestry."

Mass ended, and the makeshift church emptied. No one wanted to admit that he was in dire need of confession. I went out into the street with the others. Barbary was waiting there. He nodded to me. I nodded to Blathers, who was lingering in the doorway. Blathers turned and went to confession. Father John described Blathers' confession to me after the case was closed.

"Come in, Mr. Blathers."

"Does I has ta tell ya any sins?"

Father John thought how much fun it would be to put Blathers through the regimen of the confessional, but then he remembered that this was serious business. "Just sit down for a moment or two, so it looks like we are really having a conversation about how to save your immortal soul."

"Ah, Father, I doesn't thinks there's much chance o' savin' me soul at this point."

"My dear man, for the dangers you and your partner are facing, I am sure God is preparing a space for you in heaven this very moment."

"That's all well and good, as long as He don't 'spect me ta use it today."

Chapter 34

When Blathers emerged from the house, he didn't have a halo around his head, but he did have his hand thrust deep in his left-hand coat pocket. His right hand was also deep into his tattered right-hand pocket, holding his pistol. Somehow, the damaged pocket was still able to support the gun. He joined me in Barbary's cab, and the vehicle slowly edged its way into the neighborhood traffic.

"Is it all clear?" he asked me.

"Barbary has kept a close watch, and he hasn't seen anyone or anything suspicious."

"That's all well, but the sooner we is out o' Spitalfields the better. I has never been feelin' safe here."

No sooner had Blathers spoken than a coach and four cut in front of the cab, forcing Barbary to pull up by the side of the road. A coat of arms indicating the owner was a member of the Wesley family, was emblazoned on the door. Two robust-looking men got out and approached the cab. Blathers recognized one as having been with the Runners. He had a terrible reputation for brutality.

"We is employed by the Queen's Minister of Public Safety." The spokesman gestured toward a third man, quite different in appearance from the two hooligans who had stepped into the street. The third man was dressed expensively, in the latest fashion. His boots must have cost more than the entire ensemble of the two heavies put together.

The spokesman continued, “The minister has reason to believe ya three is involved in a conspiracy, and we is to search ya all and your coach.”

The third man said, “There is a rumor that a gang of insurrectionists is planning an attempt on the life of the Queen. We understand they have stolen a valuable piece of jewelry to help finance their plot. If we find it on you, you all shall hang.”

The two henchmen pushed Barbary and Blathers against the coach and started searching them. The first thing they found was Blathers’ revolver, which they threw on the seat of the cab. “Well, will ya look at that. The man has a revolver. That will be mine when they hang him.”

When I made an attempt to slip away, the dandy drew a pistol from beneath his cape and pointed it in my direction. “Hold where you are, or I shall save the hangman the trouble.”

****

We heard later from Mrs. Barkis that, at the Black Lion, Jenny welcomed her back. “’How was church, missus?”

“Just fine, Jenny, but I must go out again soon. Can I rely upon you to deal with the inn for a few more hours?”

“Aye, ya can. Taday be a slow day anyway. Mr. Barkis is waitin’ in the yard fer ya. He says ya asked him ta bring his cart round. Are ya goin’ fer a ride in the country, then?”

“Something like that.” Clara went out the back door of the inn, snuck into the yard through the stable, and, using a wooden box, climbed into the back of Barkis’ cart. She covered herself with a canvas tarp and said, “I’m here, Barkis. Drive on.” Barkis pulled the cart out of the yard as if he was off to a hauling job.

As they rumbled along, Clara peeked out from under the tarp to make sure they weren’t being followed.

****

“We hasn’t found nothin’.” The two roughnecks had searched Barbary, Blathers, and me thoroughly, even to the point where we each had sustained a chill by virtue of being semi-naked in the cold air. The cab had been torn apart as much as possible.

“Then it must still be with the priest. We have been duped,” the Queen’s Minister said. “Quickly, let’s get back to the house.”

The spokesman for the muscle team looked at Blathers. ”Where’s the revolver? I mean ta keep it fer me trouble.”

“It be right here in my hand. Now how would ya likes ta come and try ta get it? Ya hasn’t the authority ta steal, ya know. I is intendin’ ta protect my property, what’s the right o’ every free Englishman.”

The Minister said, “Never mind the gun. You know what we are looking for. Let’s get to it.”

****

Barbary, Blathers, and I were standing in the yard at the inn. We had reassembled the cab on the street enough to get back to the Black Lion. We were now engaged in completing the job. Blathers said, “There, now, that’s good enough for now. Here comes Clara and Barkis. Mayhap they'll stand us a refreshment."

Barkis' cart pulled into the yard with Clara placed firmly on the driver's seat next to her husband, although it wasn't possible to see him from Clara's side of the wagon. The colossal woman blocked the view of the diminutive man. She turned to him, planted a large kiss on his cheek, and said, "Thank you, Barkis, for being willing to help."

He said, "Barkis is always willin'."

****

Inside the inn, Dickens and Forster were enjoying their lunch; cheese sandwiches and pints of dark ale. "Ah, gentlemen, and the lovely Clara. Please come sit with us and tell us of your adventures."

"As ya knows, Mr. Dickens, we isn't able ta discuss matters concernin' our case, but we can say the matter o' the jewels is settled."

I raised a fist. "But the matter of the murders isn't, and it will be."

Chapter 35

"Them sandwiches looks good. What say we has a couple o' them and think things over. If we has a little somethin' ta fill our bellies, and gives some thought ta our next step, we mights avoid a beatin'."

"I don't fear a fight, but I do agree we need to have a plan on how to proceed. And we do need to eat."

"Some sandwiches, please, Clara. And I'll has one o' them pints o' ale. They looks good and refreshin'."

"And some of your lovely tea for me, please."

"Jenny will bring it right over, gents. While you are waiting, you may want to view the contents of this envelope that the lady gave me to pass on to you. She said there should be enough to finance your pursuit of Joe's murderer."

I took the envelope and looked at the contents. Blathers had some difficulty with numbers, so I was the treasurer for the partnership. I nodded to Blathers and said, "Thank you, Mrs. Barkis. Please tell the lady we appreciate her generosity."

"Well, she greatly appreciates the service you have done for her, and said if she can be of any additional help in tracking down the villains, you should just ask, through me, of course."

Dickens said, "It certainly looks like you two have had an auspicious start to your private detective business."

I replied, "The money is much needed and appreciated, but the important thing is seeing that these rogues are hanged. The life of Joe was a great cost to us."

"Mr. Forster and I agree with you and wish you all the best. If we could lend a hand we would, but, alas, in these matters we have little skill. In addition, our business at the theater awaits us, and we must hurry on. If you have a free evening, you may enjoy our play." Dickens looked at Blathers. "Of course, we will provide you with complimentary admission." Dickens and Forster sought out Clara, settled their bill, and headed off to work.

The sandwiches, ale, and tea arrived. Clara busied herself around the inn, leaving us alone to enjoy lunch and plan for the capture of a killer, or killers.

"Did ya recognize that one brute wi' Sir Little Dandy?" Blathers asked. After washing down bread and cheese with a healthy pull of ale, he sported a foam mustache.

"Is he the one that got tossed off the Runners for beating someone to death with his fists?"

"It were some time ago, but I'm sure it were him. He beat up on a feller just fer fun, thinkin' e were a queer. Turned out he were a close relative o' the royal family. He just a'scaped hangin'."

Chapter 36

The planning went on. We each added to the list of activities that might lead to the discovery of Joe's killer.

Blathers had a second pint of ale. I had a second sandwich. I guess I am one of those people who can eat nonstop without gaining a pound. Jenny attended to the lunch needs. Clara looked in from time to time, perhaps wondering if we would pay for our meal now that we had received our fee.

When we both were fully satisfied, Clara cleared the table. I paid her for the lunch.

Outside, the wind had cleared much of the fog, and the autumn sun was beginning to appear between high fluffy clouds. Blathers and I went in different directions. We had decided that I would attempt to get an interview with the Superintendent of the Metropolitan Police. I would use Sir Robert Peel's name to gain cooperation.

****

"Does ya 'as a 'pointment?" the Bobbie on duty at the gate of Scotland Yard asked. The stables were visible from the gate. I could see Pincher in his stall. The horse must have recognized me, because it began shaking its head and pawing the ground with its front hoof.

"I'm sure the Superintendent will see me, if you

ask."

"I isn't a-wastin' me time on a body what walks up wi'out a 'pointment."

I said, "Do you see how that horse knows me? You can be sure, if his horse knows me, the Superintendent knows me. If you don't go and ask, you may be in for big trouble." Pincher whinnied as if to confirm my statement.

"Aw'right, ya stands right 'ere and doesn't move. I'll goes and see." The Bobbie headed for the door that led to the head policeman's office.

I noticed a costermonger standing behind a cart of apples. He was just to the right of the gate, with his back to the wall that surrounded Scotland Yard. "I'll have two of your lovely apples." The young man wore an oversized coat with sleeves that hung down over his hands, protecting them from the cold. I gave him a few coins. His left hand emerged from the sleeve to accept the coins, which he slipped into the left-hand pocket of the tattered coat. The coins were more than the apples were worth, but I didn't ask for any change.

"Much obliged, sir," the young man said. I went back through the gate of the yard.

A few minutes later, the door of the building opened, and the guard came out into the yard accompanied by the Superintendent. "Well, where is he? Oh, there he is." I was by the stable, feeding apples to Pincher while I scratched the horse's nose. "Mr. Duff! It is nice of you to come by. Sir Robert has mentioned that you or your partner might stop. Please come in. I must be at a meeting shortly, but we can chat for about ten minutes. Cruncher, please see that Pincher is hitched to my gig. I'll be needing it in about ten minutes."

"Me name isn't Cruncher, sir. I be Bucket, sir."

"Oh. In those hats you all look alike to me. Well, anyway, get the gig ready."

"Yes, sir. I will, sir. Right away, sir."

The Superintendent ushered me into his office and pointed to a chair. "Well, what can I do for you? I understand you have had some good success in your recent adventure."

"That's true, but we do still have some unfinished business."

I told about my interest in the murders, and the Superintendent promised to share all the resources of Scotland Yard with us. Nevertheless, at the end of the interview, I felt I was no closer to catching the killer. "There is one other thing I would like to discuss with you, sir."

"Please, Mr. Duff, whatever service I may perform, ask."

"Do you know of a fellow named Caddy Quale?"

"I have heard of him, yes. He is sort of on the fringes of the law, is he not?"

"That depends on your point of view. Caddy thinks he is just easing the injustice the government inflicts on the poor, perhaps by overlooking certain taxes and the like. Nonetheless, did you know he has been arrested and is being held in Newgate?"

"I did not, and I review all of the arrest reports. Do you know which of my men arrested him?"

"It was the Queen's Minister of Public Safety. They are holding him without a hearing as a potential anarchist. I'm not a Queen's Counsel, but I do think he should get some kind of hearing."

"Do you mean to tell me that Percy Wesley arrested the man, threw him in jail, and just left him there? That's not the way we do things in England. I will certainly look into this. Now I must be off."

Chapter 37

We stepped out to the yard now filled with sunlight. Pincher was waiting, hitched to the gig. The Superintendent started to climb into the carriage. A shot rang out. A bullet grazed Pincher's withers, and the horse reared up. The Superintendent fell to the ground. A second shot sounded in the air. A bullet lodged in the driver's seat of the gig. Then someone fired a third shot.

I grabbed the reins of the frightened horse and brought him under control. The Superintendent picked himself out of the mud, while the guard cowered against the wall of the stable. And in the center of the gate, impeccably attired, smoking gun in hand, stood Sir Percy Wesley, the Queen's Minister of Public Safety. His two burly companions stood across the street with their hands thrust deep into the pockets of their coats.

"Superintendent, thank God you are uninjured. There has been an assassination attempt by conspirators. These plots grow like vermin in the filthy gin shops of Spitalfields. Fortunately, we heard of it and were able to get here in time. Our information is that your death was to be the signal for a general uprising in the slums."

I unhitched Pincher from the gig and led the horse back to his stall, where the hostler could treat the bullet wound. Then I walked deliberately past the Queen's Minister of Public Safety and looked on the street. There, face down in the middle of his wares, was the apple seller. A gun was lying among the fruit, a few inches from the right sleeve of his long coat. It seemed he had both of his hands tucked into his sleeves. I turned the dead man's head and saw a small hole. One bullet had found its rest directly between his eyes.

Chapter 38

The Superintendent, still dusting his breeches, said, "Sir Percy, you and Mr. Duff come into the office, please." By the time I got to the office, the policeman was finishing the second of two notes. "Cruncher, get in here."

The door opened and a head poked in. "I be Bucket, sir."

"Well get me Cruncher right away."

"I will, sir. Right away, sir."

A few minutes later, young Jerry Cruncher burst through the door. "Does ya wants ta see me, sir?"

"Cruncher, your coat is only half on. Where were you when I needed you?"

"I be in the loo, sir."

"Oh! Well, do you see these two envelopes?"

"I does, sir."

"The first is to my wife. Take it to her at my home. It explains why I cannot keep my appointment with her this afternoon. The second is to the Duke of Wellington. He is at the palace, so take it there. You see that I have written "Urgent" on the envelope."

"I do sees that, sir."

"Do you know what urgent means, Jerry?"

"I does, sir. It means quite impotent."

"Important, Jerry, important. Now, for blazes'

sake, button up your trousers and get these delivered."

Jerry put the envelopes on the Superintendent's desk and started for the door, grasping at his buttons with both hands.

"Jerry, don't forget the envelopes." Jerry reached for the envelopes and in doing so let go of his pants. The pants slid to the floor. He rescued the trousers, but the messages landed at my feet.

I bent at the waist and scooped them from the floor. "Here, young Jerry, I'll hold these until you're ready. Now, take your time. Be sure you have all the buttons in the right place. You need to look decent when you deliver these. You might see the Queen, you know."

When Cruncher was finally on his way, the Superintendent sat back in his chair. He crossed his legs in a relaxed fashion and said, "Well, Sir Percy, what in blazes happened out there?"

Percy Wesley smiled, a satisfied smile. "I, the Queen's Minister of Public Safety, just saved your life. Now I am going to arrest this man, as I have information he was part of the assassination plot." He pointed his pistol at me.

Chapter 39

"Sit down, Sir Percy. Nobody is arresting anybody until the Duke gets here. Then we will see what we shall see. Now, while we wait for the Duke, provide me with the details of this attempted assassination. How did you find out about it, and exactly who is behind it?"

Sir Percy, the Queen's Minister, took a chair directly in front of the Superintendent's desk. This was obviously the chair intended for the most important visitor. The most important visitor was somewhat perturbed by the policeman's interference with the performance of his duties. "I am afraid that we are wasting time here. There are dangerous things happening, and I must not allow any interference with my activities." The Queen's Minister rose from his chair and placed his hands on his hips. "You fail to understand, sir. There are people in our midst who want to overthrow the government and behead the Queen. Unless we take drastic steps, there will be a guillotine in Piccadilly Circus. We cannot be irresolute about our firmness. We must stamp out disloyalty and disagreement at every opportunity. We must strike with all of our might against those who oppose the monarchy and the established church." It sounded like a prepared political speech.

The Superintendent said, "Please sit down, Sir

Percy. I need to know the details of what just happened and just how you happened to be on the scene. Who shot at whom. Why you think Mr. Duff, here, is an insurrectionist. I also understand you have jailed some people without a hearing. I would like to know about that, as well."

"I am sorry, but there is no time to worry about these details of law. And I answer to the Queen, not to you. If you will not allow me to take this criminal into custody now, I guess there is nothing I can do. You will, however, regret this action." The very important Queen's Minister stomped out of the office.

"Well, I guess I had better start to worry. It sounds like Sir Percy has threatened me." The head of the Metropolitan Police laughed.

I said, "Thank you for keeping me out of jail. These days, once you are in Newgate, you stay in Newgate."

"I'll do my best to correct that situation, Mr. Duff."

"There is one thing I would like to show you, if you could take a moment to step outside with me."

Chapter 40

Just to one side of the Scotland Yard gate there were several Bobbies standing guard over the apple cart and its contents, including the body of the young man. Several raggedy women stood nearby crying. Behind them a crowd had gathered. The unruly throng rumbled about the shooting.

The Superintendent said, "We must get this mess cleaned up as soon as possible."

"One minute." I pointed to the gun almost touching the youth's right sleeve. "When I bought some apples from this fellow, he took the money with his left hand and put it in the left-hand pocket of his coat. If he is left-handed, then the gun should be near his left hand."

The policeman raised his eyebrows and shook his head. He asked the nearest Bobbie, "Is anyone here related to this lad?"

"Aye, sir, them ladies there. Me thinks as one o' them be 'is muther."

The Superintendent approached the grieving ladies. "Ladies, are you related to this young man?" he pointed toward the apple cart.

"This 'ere be 'is mum."

"Please accept my sincere sympathy over this tragedy. I would appreciate it if you would all step into my office, where you can be more comfortable. We need to make a brief investigation of the situation here, and then we will help you with the necessary arrangements. Could you please tell me the young man's name."

"He be Tom Green."

"Can you tell me, then, was Tom left-handed or right-handed?"

"Tom Green 'asn't got no right hand. It were cut off by one o' them Bow Street Runners when he were a wee lad."

Chapter 41

The friends, neighbors, and family of Tom Green declined the generous offer of comfort in the office of the "'ead o' them Peelers." They headed off to the nearest gin shop to treat their sorrow in their traditional manner. I, however, returned to his office with him, while, on the street, a group of Bobbies attended to the scene.

The Superintendent fell into his chair and began rubbing his forehead. "Perhaps the gun flew out of his left hand and just landed by the right hand accidentally."

"Well, sir, there is one more piece of evidence to consider. If the lad was shooting at you, he would be facing you. If he was facing you, how did Sir Percy shoot him between the eyes? He would have been standing behind the poor fellow."

"I don't know. Something is very wrong with this whole thing."

The office door opened and a handsome, well-dressed man entered. "What is this emergency?"

"Ah, my lord, please, first let me present Mr. Duff, the detective. Mr Duff, this is Arthur Wellesley, the Duke of Wellington."

"Good afternoon, Mr. Duff. Superintendent, I was in a discussion with Her Majesty when your summons arrived. What is so urgent?"

"My Lord, we may have a problem concerning your cousin."

"Percy? What has he done now?"

The Superintendent explained about what had just occurred. "Mr. Duff, using the perspicacity acquired as a member of the Bow Street Runners, pointed out some physical evidence that does not support Percy's account of the incident." He outlined my objections to the theory that Tom Green was the shooter.

He continued, "Furthermore, I am told that Percy is holding prisoners at Newgate without providing for an appearance in court. He seems to be just throwing them into gaol on suspicion and leaving them there, all very illegal."

At this point it appeared that the two men forgot my presence.

The Iron Duke rubbed his hands together. "We need to be very careful here. This is a delicate political situation. Since the Catholic Emancipation Act, certain forces have been, shall we say, very hostile to us. There is a growing fear that things English are being lost, that we need to take drastic steps to protect the realm."

"Things English *are* being lost. English *freedoms* are being lost. The right to trial is as old as the Magna Carta!" The Superintendent was turning red.

"You don't have to preach to me, sir. I know exactly how you feel, but if we lose our political position, we will be unable to do anything to protect English freedom. Being in power is what is important, and the power comes from the people, people who are afraid. We must keep them believing that if the Tories lose power they will be in danger."

"But, but!"

"Never mind the but, but. Percy is our man to remind the people that our party is serious about security."

Chapter 42

Blathers' mission was to visit Caddy Quale in Newgate. He told me about his caper with pride.

"No un 'ere goes by dat name."

"I is sure he is here. Let me look round?"

"'Elp yourself."

Blathers had been to Newgate many times before. He knew many of the gaol's residents by first name. With their help, it didn't take him long to find his man.

"Looky here. Why, yer all bruised from head ta toe. What has happened? Has ya been beaten, then?" Blathers was astounded to find Caddy huddled in a corner of the prison, sitting on a three-legged stool, wrapped in a dirty blanket.

"Faith, an' haven't I had a cordial visit from that fop Percy Wesley and his two thugs. I'm glad ya found me. According to what I been told, I am not even here. Now, isn't that a joke. Here I sit all beaten and feeling poorly, and I ain't even here. Since I ain't here, me solicitor can't see me, and I can't get out."

Blathers found another stool and sat down beside the prisoner. No doubt he began to scratch his head just above his right ear, as he always did when an idea was starting to form in his mind. "If'n ya isn't here, then they won't miss ya when ya is gone."

"Ah, faith, an' haven't those gaolers been told if

they don't keep me here they'll have their privates cut off."

"I've an idea. Sit right here till I gets back. It won't take long. I knows plenty o' the people in here." Blathers got up from his stool, removed his coat and hat, and disappeared into the depths of the prison.

****

Fewer than ten minutes passed before he was back. He had two corks from wine bottles and a small candle. Prisoners in Newgate had many of the comforts of home smuggled in by their families. They all knew it was safer to drink wine than the water available in the prison.

Blathers carefully guarded the flame as he set the candle on the stool where his fanny had previously rested. Caddy almost didn't recognize him because he was now wearing a long black coat and a top hat. In the crook of his left arm he had draped a pair of black trousers.

"Take off that there blanket and stands up, my man." Caddy did as he was bid, and Blathers held the first wine cork in the flame of the fire. Soon the Irishman's face and hands were black as, well, burnt cork, and he was dressed in the black pants, and covered by the black coat buttoned up to his throat. Blathers placed the top hat squarely on his head and said, "Follows me, now."

As they neared the gate, where the gaoler sat, Blathers signaled to Caddy that he should go ahead of him out the gate.

"Now woo's dis 'ere dat's a-goin' out o' me gate?"

Caddy turned to respond, but Blathers jumped forward in time to stop his brogue from revealing their deception.

"Why, ya silly horse, ya. This here is the undertaker's new man. Wasn't ya awake when he comes in?"

"Now, ya knows dis man does ya, Blathers?" Of course the gatekeeper wasn't sure he hadn't dozed off at some point during his shift. At the very least he had stepped over to the wall to relieve himself more than once.

Blathers vouched for the black man, who still restrained from speaking. "I does. I were just down ta the undertaker the other day, and I seen this here feller there."

"Gets along den, da two o' ya, and leaves me be."

Caddy took ten steps outside the prison, looked back, saw that Blathers was right behind him, leapt in the air, and clicked his heels.

"Keep a movin' then. We isn't outta the woods yet. Gets ya up ta the corner. Barbary should be there."

At the gate of Newgate, the gaoler stood scratching his head with one hand and feeling his testicles with the other. Maybe he remembered Percy Wesley's threat and wondered if all his parts would be in place the next day.

Chapter 43

Caddy Quale, in his disguise as an undertaker's assistant, started to open the door to Barbary's cab. "Hey, ya darky, ya can't ride in this cab."

"Saints preserve us, don't ya be knowing your own good friend and employer, now, ya sassy man, ya."

Barbary wasn't sure he heard Caddy's voice coming out of the black man trying to get in his cab, but Blathers was right behind him. He gave Caddy a shove onto the seat, and yelled, "Make for the Black Lion. Quick!"

Barbary jerked the reins, and the cab set off toward the center of London. The route led back past the prison, where the gatekeeper had already fallen asleep in a chair tilted against the end of the prison wall, apparently contented that all of his body parts were safe.

Chapter 44

When I returned from Scotland Yard, Dickens and Forster were enjoying a late meal. Blathers, Barbary, and Quale joined us soon thereafter. Clara Barkis was managing the establishment from her chair, where she could converse with her guests while also keeping a close watch on Jenny. The only one not present was Barkis, himself. "He's off carting again," Clara announced as she raised her pint jar to her mouth.

Caddy came through the door first, but no one recognized him. Mrs. Barkis struggled to pull her fanny out of the chair and prevent an unwanted patron from entering. "Have you come into the wrong place?" she asked.

"Faith, me dear Clara, is the disguise so good, now, you don't even recognize Caddy Quale when ya see him?"

Blathers and Barbary were right behind Caddy. Blathers said, "Takes it easy now, Clara. We has had quite a time of it, hasn't we. What we needs from you is some soap and water, right after the drinks is served."

Clara sat back down, but it took some time for the fanny flab to rise up her sides and spill over the chair arms so she was again comfortable. She signaled for Jenny to take a drink order. Dickens asked the girl, "Where is the lovely Liz today?"

"Ah, she only does the nights, now Jane is gone, I does fer them what comes in during the daytime, now. Doesn't ya like me, Mr. Dickens?"

"My dear Jenny, I just love you. I will have to lunch here every day from now on, just because you are here." He started to reach for her derriere.

But with a quick move she avoided his hand, swished her skirt in his direction, smiled, and said, "I'll be pleased ta serves ya on any day, Mr. Dickens." As the writer had lost his balance in the missed attempt, and was now on his knees, he could only grunt. Forster found the situation quite amusing and asked, "Have you also decided that it is appropriate to take your meals from the floor, Charles?"

In fact, everyone was laughing except Caddy and me. Laughing made the results of the Irishman's beating hurt more. I wasn't laughing because I still wasn't able to find any humor in this cruel world.

Chapter 45

"Ah! Look at my partner there. Duff, we has got the jewels back, and we has got Caddy Quale outa Newgate. Time is we enjoys ourselves some."

"There will be no enjoyment for me until Joe's killer is made to answer for his crime."

"Sure, an' don't I agree with Duff. Me man from Dublin was brutally murthered, probably by the same person, and I want that man found." Caddy was rubbing his left shoulder with his right hand. "Faith, an' them gaolers know how ta smack a man so he remembers it." He winced as he moved in his chair.

I said, "I had best tell of the incident I witnessed at Scotland Yard." I told of the alleged attempt to assassinate the Superintendent of Police, the part played by Percy Wesley and his henchmen, and the shooting of the costermonger. "Of course, the physical evidence makes me doubt the poor fellow was involved in any way except to take a bullet and the blame. I presented this to the Superintendent, and he informed the Duke, right there in front of me. But I don't think they will take any action. Seems there is some political reason they can't. You know, of course, the little dandy is the Duke's cousin."

Caddy, still nursing his wounds, said, "Well, now we have three murthers ta deal with, perhaps all by the same hand."

Blathers and I, Dickens and Forster, Barbary, and Clara all paused to consider the ramifications of Caddy's theory. During this pause, Jenny whispered something into her mistress's ear.

"Oh, my!" Clara had started to wiggle out of her chair, when a man and a woman entered the room. "Gentlemen, we are relying on your ability to block this meeting from your mind. My lady needs to speak to you all without further delay, but her appearance here, with me, must never be known by anyone outside this room." Dickens and Forster gave Father John and the lady their chairs.

The lady began, "My husband has told me about the attack outside police headquarters and the murder of one more unfortunate citizen. He has also told me he and the Duke of Wellington are unable to act for political reasons. This young upstart, the Duke's cousin, has the Queen, much of Parliament, and a large portion of voters frightened to death. He keeps claiming we are on the verge of a revolution such as occurred in France not all that long ago."

Forster said, "There is a great deal of agitation among the lower middle classes. The Reform Act and the Emancipation Act helped to release some of the pressure, but it's a bit lucky the shooting of the costermonger didn't start something."

The lady sought more aid. "I have told my husband and the Duke of the murder of Mr. Quale's man and of poor Joe. They believe these deaths, as well as that of the fruit seller were the work of Percy Wesley and his brutal men. Unfortunately, they are unable to do anything to stop this dangerous upstart. They need your help in thwarting his plans to rule by fear."

Caddy Quale asked, "Faith, now, an' does Sir Robert have any plan for us?"

Father John responded, "His only statement was that we should tell you all to do your best to keep from getting killed yourselves."

Chapter 46

The lady, wanting to get away before her presence was discovered, left the Black Lion with a wish of "God bless you all."

She gave a fat envelope to Clara.

Father John stayed on.

All of us in the taproom scratched our heads. That is, all except Caddy. He still hurt too much to be able to lift a hand to his head.

"Well," Dickens said, "that certainly places the onus on some of us. For myself, I am willing to help in any way I can, but my forte is writing. I'm not good at physical things."

Forster said, "Don't worry about the physical things, Charles. I'm sure we will find someone to care for that part of the operation."

Blathers asked, "Does ya has some idea about how we's ta go about gettin' these fellers? If'n ya does, I fer one would be glad ta hear it."

Forster was the planner and organizer of most of the successful enterprises he and Dickens enjoyed. "I think the first step is to identify our resources."

"What resources?" I asked. "We haven't any resources."

"We would if'n we had that gig and Pincher," Blathers said.

"Oh! I forgot to tell you, Blathers. Pincher got shot during the attack on the Superintendent."

"Them bastards shot Pincher? I'll kills them wi' me bare hands, I will." Blathers' ire added to the ruddiness of his complexion.

"Now, don't get upset," I went on. "It was only a flesh wound. The animal is in the good care of the Superintendent's hostler. He'll be fine."

"In my way o' thinkin', there's no excuse fer shootin' a poor animal. These is the worst of rascals."

Barbary added, "I agree wi' Blathers. The poor horses always get the worst of them kinds of fracases."

Forster regained control of the discussion. "Indeed, it seems you all have a reason for exacting revenge on these people, but just being angry won't get any results. Again, I think we need to begin to consider how we should proceed. And before you go off on a discussion of how to treat horses, let me tell you what our resources are."

We all sat quietly, listening to Forster.

"First and foremost, we have a group of individuals with a variety of talents. We should plan how to best use them. For example, Dickens wouldn't be much help in any physical conflict. If a fight broke out one would find him a liability instead of an asset. On the other hand, Blathers and Duff have experience in the ways of using force. You see, we need to plan a way to make sure we get the most out of the abilities of each of us."

Blathers said, "I sees the plan will be fer yas all ta sit here and sip brandy while me and Duff is out in the street gettin' all beat up."

Dickens said, "I think Forster is correct. I would be more likely to get injured out there than either of you.

Although I'll admit, it sounds like there is a good chance someone else is going to get killed."

Chapter 47

The discussion over who could do what best, and who would be in the most danger continued until everyone was assigned a role. “But we still doesn’t has a plan,” Blathers pointed out.

Forster stroked his chin. “Indeed, I think there is one more element we need before we can decide on a definite plan.”

“Faith, an’ now what might that be, Mr. Forster?” Caddy Quale asked.

“Bait! We need to have something that will make these fellows so bold they will make a mistake, an error that will be evident to many, and will be such that everyone will find it abhorrent.”

“What does abhorrent mean?” I asked.

Dickens answered, “Something so awful that everyone will get damn mad.” This was one of the few times Dickens had participated in the conversation. He was busy writing in his notebook.

Forster asked, “What in the devil are you doing, Charles?”

“Oh, I’m just making some notes. This is good stuff.”

Blathers said, “Never ya minds that. Let’s gets back ta the bait and the plan.” Instead of scratching his head, he stroked his neck under his chin with two fingers; a universal gesture of thirst. Then the door opened, and Barkis, himself, came in.

"Well, what a fine gatherin' we has here. Will ya all has a drink on the house? Jenny, drinks fer our guests, if'n ya please."

Chapter 48

Forster took a long drink from his pint of bitter before he started again. “Did you say earlier that the pearls had been returned to the lady, Blathers?”

“I did. Clara can tell us that.”

“Yes they have, Mr. Forster.”

“I think the pearls would make fine bait. Do our adversaries know they are no longer missing?”

“We doesn’t know. Them fellers tried ta gets them on quite a few ’casions, but we has outfoxed them. Maybe they doesn’t knows it as yet.”

Forster rubbed his chin. “How did they find out about the necklace in the first place?”

“I am afraid that is my fault,” Father John admitted. “Didn’t this all start when I was giving instructions in the faith to Lady Peel. The house in Spitalfields has long been used for the other work of the Church among the Irish in the neighborhood. It is equipped with a priest’s hole, a place where priests would hide in times of persecution. When the attack on the house began, I rushed the lady out the back to her carriage. Of course, I couldn’t be seen riding with her. Benjamin, the man Caddy had assigned to guard me, went to confront the attackers. I ducked into the priest’s hole. When the noise stopped, didn’t I look out, and Benjamin was on the floor. I ran to him to help, but it was too late.

"Wasn't it then I noticed the lady's reticule on the floor beside the chair where she was sitting. As I picked it up, the door opened, and a constable peeked in. It was the same fellow that was later guarding the house."

Blathers said, "Ah, Young Jerry Cruncher. How did he finds out what was in the bag?"

"He saw the body and wouldn't come into the place. I went out, and he demanded to see what was in the bag. He saw the necklace. He must have somehow let information about the necklace out of the bag, so to say."

"Priests isn't 'posed ta make jokes," Blathers said.

Forster placed his finger next to his nose and said, "Indeed, this is a serious matter, Father, but a little levity is always good for the soul, is it not."

Dickens looked up from his notebook. "Anyway, the question is, can we make these scoundrels believe the pearls are still missing."

Chapter 49

The meeting finally ended. All heads nodded in agreement, and Dickens wrote with gusto in his notebook, mumbling, "Good stuff, good stuff." Blathers and I finished our beverages and set out to visit Scotland Yard.

****

Jerry Cruncher was on duty at the gate. As we approached the constable, I said, "This should be fun and save some time."

"What is it ya fellers wants, then? Ya can't just walks into Scotland Yard likes ya owns the place, donch ya see."

Blathers said, "Ah, Young Jerry, me boy. That's a nice hat ya has there. Handsome thing, isn't it, Duff? Don't ya worry, Young Jerry. We is just here ta visit Pincher. Duff tells me some ragamuffin shot the poor horse. He's me favorite animal in all the world, ya knows."

I added, "Why don't you come with us while we see the horse, Jerry? That fellow over there can watch the gate, and you can be sure we aren't up to something."

"That's a very good ideer. Bucket, watch the gate whiles I goes wi' these fellers, will ya now."

Blathers had already found Pincher's stall and was

feeding him an apple. Jerry and I joined him. "The animal be well taken care for, donch ya see," Jerry said.

I said, "He looks lovely, all things considered. By the way, Jerry, you remember the fellow in the black coat that was hanging around the house in Spitalfields?"

"I does."

"Had you ever seen him before the time he walked up to you, after Blathers and I had searched the house?"

Jerry looked at me with suspicion. "Why does ya asks, Mr. Duff?"

"Well, looking back on that day, when we saw you talking to him, it seemed you knew who he was."

"Why, yes. 'E were the feller what were in the 'ouse when I finds the body there."

"Did he take anything away from the house, maybe a clue?"

"I doesn't knows 'bout no clue. 'E were carryin' a bag wi' 'im when 'e goes out o' the 'ouse."

"Did you see what was in the bag?"

"I did." Jerry was now looking away from me, trying to be evasive. Blathers just continued to stroke the horse like he wasn't interested in the conversation.

"What was in the bag, Jerry? Was there a pearl necklace in it?"

"'Ow does ya knows that?"

"Oh, we have our ways. Did you know the necklace is still missing? But Blathers and I have a very good lead. We expect to find it today, or tomorrow at the latest. Well, Blathers, are you satisfied that Pincher is being well cared for?"

"I is. Nice talkin' wi' ya again, Young Jerry."

Chapter 50

The next stop was the gin shop in Spitalfields. Hugh Conway was at the door. “Ah, ’tis dem rouzzers. I t’ought dat your business in dis neighborhood was done, now.”

“Now, Hugh, we has told ya we is no longer wi’ the police. Don’t be callin’ us rozzers, or the whole place will be atter us.”

“Den, what is ya doin’ here?”

I said, “We want to ask you if you have heard anything about some jewelry, a pearl necklace, to be more exact.”

“Ah sure, ’twas just last night dat all the ladies came wearing pearl necklaces, don’t ya know. We’re very strict ’bout how our customers be dressed. Where da ya t’ink ya are, at da palace?”

“Now, Hugh,” Blathers continued, “we is interested in a particular necklace, isn’t we. All we is askin’ is if ya knows anythin’ about this here necklace what we is seekin’, then we would ’preciate your help, that’s all.”

“Da lads dat come in here wouldn’t know a pearl from a cobblestone. If’n dey had some pearls, dey’ed give dem ta da wee ones ta play wit’.”

I said, “So you haven’t heard anything. Can we get you to ask around on our behalf? If you can provide us with some information, we will make it worth your while, if you get my meaning."

"If'n I get anythin' of value to ya, we'll discuss how much it be worth afore ya hear 'bout it, if'n ya get my meanin'."

Chapter 51

There was one more stop, the house in Spitalfields. But before we could return there we needed to allow a little time to pass, and there were a couple of errands to run. We stopped at Blathers' rooms, and Blathers picked up his revolver and some additional bullets. "Here, Duff, puts this in your pocket." He handed me his cudgel. "Ya doesn't know when ya will be needin' somethin' like this, now does ya." I pocketed the weapon, and we headed out for the Black Lion.

Blathers asked, "Is we being followed?"

"I think so. But we will know for sure when we get back to the Lion. Barbary is back there somewhere. He'll spot anyone on our tail."

****

Charles Dickens had left by the time Blathers and I returned to the inn. He had a past due deadline. He needed to finish his story and mollify his editor, or he'd gain a reputation for being tardy with his work. The rest of the team, however, was waiting patiently for reports from their field operators, Blathers and me, and Barbary.

Barkis, himself, joined our group. Forster assigned him two jobs. His first charge was providing beverages as required. "Who's gonna pays fer these here drinks, is whats I want ta know."

Clara answered, "Never you mind, love. You just keep track of what is consumed, and I'm quite certain my lady will see us good for it." Barkis found a chalkboard and began tallying the drinks.

His second job was to provide needed tools. He obtained them from his own stock, the tools he used to maintain the inn and to repair his dray as needed. Right now the plan called for two crowbars. They sat on the table in the taproom.

We had just made ourselves comfortable when Barbary joined the group. Blathers asked, "Was we bein' followed?"

"Aye, dere were one o' dem 'oods on your tail. Me thinks it were one o' da ones what jumped ya da other day. Dat Percy feller, 'e must 'as a small army, 'e must."

Forster said, "Well, you are being followed. That's good. Now let's go over the next part of the plan and get going on it. Clara, do you have the item for Mr. Duff?"

"Here you are. I put it in this wrapping so no one would see it until you wanted them to." I stuffed the parcel into the left-hand pocket of my coat. The cudgel was in the right-hand pocket.

"Now that the props are distributed," Forster said, "everyone recite your part in this little drama for me."

Chapter 52

Blathers and I loaded our tools into Barbary's cab and jumped in behind. Barbary cracked the whip and headed to Spitalfields.

At the little house where it all started, we carried the tools through the front door. Anyone who was watching could see them. The house remained unlocked. We removed our coats and put them on one of the few chairs that had survived the attack earlier in the week. Barbary drove off to the sound of crowbars ripping up boards.

It wasn't long before Blathers stopped tearing up the floor, wiped the sweat from his brow, and said, "Ah, this be hard work, ya know. How long does ya thinks we need ta go on?"

I said, "Until we've convinced them."

"I wishes they'd hurry up. Does ya think they is too dumb ta gets the idea?"

"Just be patient. I think they are too smart to jump into a possible trap without waiting to see what's going to happen. Keep making noise, and soon it'll get to them."

"'Tis when we stops banging round they'll wants ta know what it is that's happenin'."

"Maybe your right. Let's try something." I went across the room to where I had left my coat. I retrieved the parcel Clara had given me, unwrapped it, and took the contents, the lady's reticule, to the window as if to examine it in the light. I glanced out the window but didn't see anyone. I went back into the room, and as I was wondering if Forster's plan was going to work, I heard the rear door squeak. In a short second Percy Wesley was in the doorway with a cocked pistol in each hand.

Chapter 53

Percy said the obvious, "Don't move, either of you. This place is surrounded by my men with orders to shoot to kill if either of you leave the building."

Blathers glanced at me. I was almost smiling. But the dandy with the pistols was serious. There was definitely a tension in his voice, and he continued to wave the loaded pistols at us. "I want that necklace, and I want it now." He waved the guns some more.

Blathers said, "Now, hold on there, afore ya hurts a body. Ya doesn't wants ta shoot now, do ya?"

"I'll shoot if you don't hand over that bag. Now!"

I held the bag out in front of me. "Here it is. Do you want me to toss it to you?"

"Just put it on the chair, where your coat is."

I put the bag down. "Now get back against that far wall, both of you." Wesley kept the guns on us while he sidestepped toward the chair. When he reached the chair he put one pistol in his coat pocket and jammed his hand into the reticule. It came out empty. He pulled the pistol from his pocket and again leveled both guns at us. "Where is it? You thieves! You have it hidden on you. If you don't turn it over right now, I'll take it from your dead bodies."

Blathers raised his right hand, palm out as if to stop traffic. "Now, hold on. Ya won't finds it on us, and ya won't finds it wi'out us. We is in business, ya know. We is private investigators. That means we is able ta works fer the one what we wants ta work fer, the one what pays the most, do ya see."

I added, "Blathers is right. We can't live on our honor. We need cash to keep ourselves alive. And we know where the necklace is. Do you want to bid?" I tried to maintain a businesslike tone, showing no fear. "We know what the others are paying. Of course, in your case, the price includes a guarantee of our continued good health. And we will take that and the possibility of future employment into consideration."

"How do I know you have the pearls? If you have them, what are you doing here, tearing up the floor?"

"We has the bag, doesn't we?"

"But what have you been searching for here?"

"We has been searchin' fer a chance ta talk ta you wi'out them others knowin' about it."

Wesley went to the front door and kicked backwards. The door opened, and the two primary henchmen entered the room. "Keep those two covered while I think." The two bullies came farther into the room and pushed Blathers and me into a corner.

"Now, take it easy. We just mights be one o' you any minute now."

The larger and more aggressive of the two just grunted and shoved Blathers again.

Percy, still standing with his chin in his hand said, "Are you suggesting you would hand over the necklace if I were to make you part of my," he hesitated, "organization?"

I responded, "Let's just say that Sir Robert didn't make us a very good offer when we worked for the

Peelers."

"Aye, we has had ta go round breakin' up book stores fer them do-gooders ta keeps from starvin'. We doesn't like doin' that, but we does likes ta eat."

"What kind of work are you willing to do?"

"We could replace them two dummies right there," Blathers said. "By the way, what's it ya calls that thug?" He pointed at the one who was doing the pushing.

"Tope, stop pushing people. His name is Tope."

"If'n ya was ta asks me, it should be dope." Tope started in Blathers' direction again, but Wesley yanked him back by the shoulder.

I added, "Yes, those two certainly didn't handle the murder of the costermonger very well. A person would have to be very stupid to believe a man with his hand missing could have shot the gun with his stump."

Wesley looked at his men. "You mean they tried to frame a man that couldn't have been an assassin?" He shook his head in disbelief.

"Everyone from the poor lad's kin to your cousin the Duke knew he hadn't shot the gun."

Tope said, "Kills dem now! Dem be notten but trouble."

"Shut up, you nitwit. Maybe this would be easier if you two waited outside."

Tope gave Blathers another shove, hard enough so he lost balance and fell against the wall. I moved toward the belligerent ape, but Wesley yelled, "Stop that!" I stopped, happy this hasty movement did not get me smacked by the monster.

"You two morons get outside and wait until I call, understand? I think it is about time we got someone with brains on our side."

Blathers said, "With all this openin' and closin' o' that door, I'm a gettin' cold." He moved toward the chair where his coat was lying under mine. "Here, Duff, put on your coat. Ya doesn't wants ta get a chill, now. Ya knows how ya gets them sniffles all the time."

Both of us put on our coats and put our hands in the pockets.

Wesley said, "Let's go to my office and talk about your joining with me."

"Right!" Blathers said. "But we needs ta make it looks like we is under arrest or whatever ya calls it. We doesn't wants ta give a'body any idea we is in yer ga-, yer organization, just yet, if ya sees me point."

"You're right. Very good point. Here, I have my pistols on you. Just move ahead and get into my carriage."

Chapter 54

Percy Wesley's carriage took us past Scotland Yard and down a side street. In front of the Yard, Young Jerry guarded the gate, waiting for another big case to demand his attention. As the carriage bearing the Wesley coat of arms passed, Young Jerry saluted. "Good man, that constable," Wesley said.

Two streets southwest of the Yard we turned into a narrow alley; then we turned through an open gate into a stable area surrounded by a high wall. A gig carrying Tope and his partner followed. Tope was driving. The other thug jumped from the carriage and closed the heavy gates.

We got out of our carriage. Wesley still had his pistols trained on us. "This is for the benefit of my ignorant associates," he explained. "We can talk in my office." He pointed toward the building at the rear of the stable yard with his guns.

Inside the office, the most prominent feature was a large map of the world. Much of the area on several continents was shaded in red. The east coast of North America was in black. Wesley said, "Do you see this? The area in red is the British Empire, the greatest empire the world has ever seen. It is our destiny to be rulers and bring Christianity and civilization to the entire world."

"What's the black part, then?" Blathers asked.

"That is what I am trying to guard against. Those are the colonies we have lost because we were not firm in our resolve, not firm in two wars. There are people among us who would weaken our position in the world. They are unwilling to stand up for our destiny. They are unwilling to engage in confrontation with the enemies of the Crown and the established church.

"Catholic emancipation is a good example. In order to avoid a little difficulty in Ireland, Sir Robert and the Duke allowed that act to pass. The cowards, they call themselves Tories. Bah!"

Blathers and I were taken aback by Percy Wesley's heated speech. I said, "Of course, there are certain rights that all Englishmen should enjoy at any cost. Maybe Sir Robert and the Duke are just trying to be democratic."

"Democratic! Democracy is a lot of balderdash. People don't want rights. They just want to know they won't have their heads chopped off. That's what I will give them when I get rid of the weak-kneed Tories and the bleeding-heart Liberals. I'll keep order throughout the Empire, and the Queen and the Archbishop of Canterbury will be my biggest supporters."

Neither Blathers nor I said a word.

Wesley said, "Well, now you know where I stand. Do you want to work for me and my great cause, or not?"

Blathers answered, "Why, sure we does. We wants ta be friends o' the Queen and o' the Archbishop too. Doesn't we, Duff?"

"We certainly do. Put us down for any job."

"The first job is to take down Sir Robert and gain

control of the Metropolitan Police. The necklace will be evidence that he can't control his own wife. Nobody wants a cuckold in charge of the safety of the nation."

Chapter 55

"We doesn't has ta deal wi' that dope Tope, does we?"

"Tope is just a muscle man. It is quite obvious he has no brains. If he gives you any trouble, let me know, but feel free to use his muscle in any way you deem fit."

I said, "Then our first job is to get the necklace and see that it gets into your hands. Do you think you would like to be there when it is turned over to us?"

"Will my presence be necessary?"

"Well," Blathers reasoned, "if'n you're on the scene, ya can be sure nothing will happen 'tween the time we gets the jewels and the time ya gets them." We were counting on the probability that Wesley still did not trust us. "Ya might even bring along them gorillas. We mights be able ta use them, but I doesn't wants them round 'less ya's there ta control them."

"How will I know when you will be obtaining the necklace?"

I explained, "We'll let you know in plenty of time. You and Tope and the other fellow just wait until you hear from us. It should be tomorrow some time."

"I'll be there. Do you know where the location will be?"

"We're quite sure it will be in Spitalfields. There is

a house there we know of as a safe house. We think the other party will be willing to meet us at this location. We'll send a messenger with the time and place as soon as we have it all set."

"There is another person involved, then?"

"Oh, yes! He is quite willing to work with us, but he needs to be careful. He is a wanted man in several places. And we have heard there's a grand reward for his capture, dead or alive. He must believe he will be safe, or he will not dare to come."

"One other thing," Blathers added, "It might be wise ta has Tope and his mate comes in't the house 'head o' ya. That way we has the ability ta show the other feller he hasn't ta fear, and he won't back out on us, do ya see."

Wesley snickered. "I thought you were afraid of Tope."

"We isn't 'fraid o' nobody. Tope and the other goon is just stupid, that's all. Wi' ya on the scene, we is sure they won't do any o' their dumb tricks. If'n I was ya, I'd take them guns away so's they doesn't accidentally shoot a body."

Chapter 56

Caddy Quale's job was to make arrangements for the house. He owned several houses in Spitalfields, some rented and some used for emergencies. Evictions were common among the Irish in the neighborhood. Illness resulting from the long hours of hard labor in the mills was the major cause of being unable to pay the rent. Rather than have a deserving family living on the streets, Caddy would make one of his emergency houses available.

For this emergency there was a perfect house. It was next to Hugh Conway's gin shop, not far from the house where the pearls were originally lost. The main entrance was on an alley that ran between the house and the gin shop, the same alley where Blathers and I first employed Joe. In contrast to many of the neighborhood alleys, Caddy Quale's employees kept this one clean. The entrance to the house was about five feet above street level, so there were stone steps leading to the door in the middle of the wall, several yards away from the main thoroughfare.

But providing the house wasn't Quale's only job. Suffering from his injuries, he found it difficult to get around; nevertheless, part of his task was to make certain other arrangements. With the help of Barbary, he was able to return to his residence and assemble his part of the cast.

Father John's assignment required him to engage in some delicate diplomacy. He hoped he could rely on his training at a Jesuit seminary to enable him to accomplish his task. He needed to play the part of a clergyman. But could he put on a white collar and convince someone he was something other than a Catholic? He had to. It was critical to the success of the plot.

Contacting the relatives of the costermonger who was shot outside Scotland Yard was also his responsibility.

Forster went to look for Dickens, to see if he could provide an additional element. He told me of his chat with the writer at the theater in Drury Lane. "Why, certainly, John." Dickens had told him. "I'm finished here, and I'll go over to Fleet Street right now. Please write down the address for me. You say it's the house right next to the gin shop on the corner. I'm sure that we will find it."

"We? Will you accompany your friends?"

"You know I couldn't miss a scene such as you have described. I'll be there with pen in hand."

****

At half nine the next morning, the whole team once again gathered at the Black Lion. Dickens attended. Mr. and Mrs. Barkis served strong tea and cornbread. Alcohol was not available. Forster went over the details and checked to see that each one had completed his or her assignment. "Father John, the costermonger's family has agreed to cooperate?"

"They have. Someone has already been to the undertaker to make the arrangements."

"It isn't too late to use the lad, is it?"

"Because of the cold weather, we will be all right for today. I believe the delivery has been made already, has it not, Caddy?"

"Yes, haven't me and Barbary been to the house early this morning, and isn't all the staff and their equipment waiting right now."

"Charles, how about your friends?"

"Barbary has arranged for a cab for us all. Your cousin, is it, Barbary?"

"'Tis me second cousin, sir. Meself and me first cousin is providin' transport fer da Father and his group."

Forster declared, "Indeed, it looks like all is ready. Let us begin."

I said, "We have a messenger waiting outside. Here is our note to Wesley. It says to meet us at the house at noon. We tell him to be sure he is not early, so he doesn't scare off our contact."

Forster asked, "Did he ask you who your contact was?"

Blathers said, "Good show he didn't. We didn't remembers ta cover that point. But we does remind him in the note ta sends in them two monkeys a'fore he come in hisself."

Forster said, "I hope we haven't forgotten to cover any other points. Does anyone have anything that needs to be dealt with now?"

Everyone was silent except Clara, who after a moment said, "God bless you all."

Chapter 57

Each of the cast that had a job outside of the house set out. Later reports made me believe their activities went something like the following.

After Father John went into the Barkis' private rooms and changed costumes, Barbary drove him to the offices of the Society for the Suppression of Vice. There he presented his credentials as a priest of the established church of Ireland, complete with a document from the Archbishop of Canterbury identifying him as a bishop. This bishop, two other clergymen, and four large-busted ladies enjoyed tea and small cakes. Barbary waited outside with his cab. While he waited, a second cab pulled up behind him. Barbary got down off his seat, as did the second driver.

"Tank ye fer comin', cousin," Barbary said. "Dey'll be out 'bout half eleven. Dat should gets us ta da scene just as da action starts. Timin' be important, ya knows."

****

In Fleet Street, Dickens jumped down from yet another cab. "I'll be but a moment. I need to collect a few fellows in here. You are Barbary's cousin, then?"

"I be 'is second cousin, gov. They calls me Jingle. Donch ya worry now. I be right 'ere when ya is ready."

"Jingle. I've heard that name somewhere before.

Well, thank you, Jingle. I won't be long. We certainly do not want to miss this performance. I understand the curtain will go up at exactly noon." Within five minutes he was back with three young rowdy fellows. They piled into Jingle's cab and passed around a flask as they started toward Spitalfields.

****

Blathers and I were already on stage. Barbary had dropped us at the house in Spitalfields before setting out to provide transportation to Father John and his companions. We met the rest of the cast assembled by Caddy Quale. Caddy and John Forster were on hand, as well. They, however, were not actors. Caddy was acting as producer and Forster was director. As soon as Act I started, they would have to be unseen by anyone. But when Blathers and I came through the door they were both busy with the arrangements. Caddy called us to a corner of the room where two young women, clothed only in their underwear, were standing. "Blathers and Duff, these two young ladies are, shall we say, business acquaintances of mine. This is Nell and this is Betty."

The girls curtsied, holding aside skirts that weren't there. Nell said, "We is pleased ta meech ya." I felt flushed. Blathers ogled.

Quale said, "You understand the part that the girls play. Even though they are experienced professionals, they should not be required to provide any services that are not part of the plan."

I, still feeling somewhat warm, said, "Oh, yes, we understand." It seemed that Blathers wasn't sure he could remember the details of the plan.

As noon drew near, Forster gathered the group together. "Indeed, I believe you all know your parts.

Nell and Betty, you are sure of what you should do?"

"Donch ya worries 'bout us. We done this kind'a t'ing all our lives. Well, since we was twelve, anyway." Nell wiggled her hips. Betty straightened her hose, rubbing her hands up and down her legs. She winked at Blathers as though she knew him from somewhere.

Forster said, "Blathers, you and Duff should go out now. Blathers! Blathers do you hear me?"

My partner shook his head as though to wake himself from a trance. His face reddened. "Oh, yes, yes. We is a-goin' now. Come on, there, Duff. Pays attention ta what's happenin'."

I raised my eyebrows, shrugged my shoulders, and followed Blathers up the stairway to the next floor. We went down a back stair, two stories, to the main floor of the building, where a door opened onto the back street. We hurried down the street behind the gin shop just as Barbary and his first cousin pulled their cabs to the side of the road. Blathers and I went around the corner and turned at the next corner again. Then, as we passed the gin shop, our pace slowed. We turned into the alley and climbed the steps to the main entrance of the house. We knew someone watched from a coach parked opposite the gin shop. We knocked. John Forster let us in.

Forster continued to set the stage. "Very good, then. The final piece of business is to bring in the last prop. Is it here, Caddy?"

Caddy went to a closet in a back corner of the room. He opened the door, and the body of the slain costermonger tumbled onto the floor.

Chapter 58

"Just leave him there. The position is perfect. Now, everyone, just a reminder, this is the stairwell to the upper floor. Quale and I will be there in case something goes wrong. It is also where you make your entrances and exits. Now, places, everyone."

Forster and Quale went up the stairs. The scantily clad ladies squeezed into a corner in the front of the room where they would not be seen by someone coming through the door. I too stood near the front of the room where I could also see the street. Blathers stood near the open door, revolver in hand. The noon bell sounded.

Two men crossed the street, heading for the steps to the house. A smaller man loitered across from the gin shop near the parked coach.

At the end of the road, Barbary's second cousin was parking his cab, full of half intoxicated newspapermen and Charles Dickens. I saw Dickens speak and imagined he said, "Steady now, lads. I have promised you the story of the decade. You had best be able to remember what has happened. This way."

On the road at the other end of the alley, Barbary and his first cousin were discharging their passengers. Barbary drove the clergymen. His first cousin carried the buxom ladies of the Committee for the Suppression of Vice. As they stepped on the unpaved road, the ladies all held perfumed hankies to their noses and looked about with disgust and disbelief at the squalor.

The clergymen, all but Father John, also appeared to be amazed that such terrible living conditions existed within a short drive of their own parishes. Father John pointed toward the house, and they all followed him.

As they neared, I heard one of the fat ladies yell, "Hallelujah!"

Meanwhile the thugs kicked the mud from their boots on the first of the stone steps and climbed to the door. Tope tried the door, found it unlocked, and slowly pushed it open. He stuck his head in, and Blathers fired his pistol. The bullet hit the wall above the door. Tope jumped backward and knocked down his partner. They both regained their composure as Percy Wesley, the Queen's Minister of Public Safety, sprinted across the muddy street and up the stone steps. "Out of my way, you fools." He pushed his two henchmen aside and, with a pistol in each hand, kicked open the door.

Chapter 59

"Do come in, ducky." Nell popped out of the stairwell and grabbed Wesley by the neckcloth. One pistol discharged into the ceiling as she reached down and unbuttoned the front of his pants. He dropped the second pistol as Betty yanked his pants down from behind.

By the time Tope and his associate gained control of themselves, after having fallen all over each other again at the sound of Wesley's pistol shot, Wesley was on the floor with his pants around his ankles. Nell sat on his chest with her legs posed in a very unladylike manner. Betty sat back to back with Nell. She had her knees raised somewhat higher than her shoulders. She placed her feet well apart so what little clothing she was wearing stretched provocatively. She rubbed the insides of Wesley's naked thighs. All this time the body of the costermonger lay quietly in the corner by the cupboard. And Percy Wesley clung to his recently fired pistol.

Immediately behind Tope and his mate, the most fully endowed of the ladies from the Society for the Prevention of Vice rushed in. "You hussies!" she yelled. She raised her umbrella over her head. The girls jumped like frogs in a lily pond and hid behind Tope's massive form. The umbrella came down on Wesley's right shoulder as he was attempting to pull up his pants.

He fell back to the floor, exposing all he possessed to the Vice lady.

"Hallelujah!"

Now two of her companions came into formation behind her. One of them uttered a less exuberant "hallelujah," followed by "Oh, my!"

"I know you!" one of the other ladies shouted. As the others looked askance at her, she corrected herself. "I mean, I know your face. You are the Duke of Wellington's cousin. Shame on you, consorting with the likes of these." She pointed to Betty and Nell as they were making their exit, stage right, through the door to the stairway.

Just in time to see the girls disappear, the newspaper reporters pushed their way into the room. Nell, delayed her exit to give one of them a wink. He waved sheepishly. His comrade behind him noticed the exchange. "Ah, you know Nell. Do you know her friend, Betty? They are a lovely team."

"Look here," the first reporter said, "a murdered man, and there's Percy Wesley with his pants off and a pistol in his hand."

The young men of the press had seen enough and hurried to get out of the room and meet their deadlines. On the other hand, the ladies from the Vice Society were just warming up. They were putting their umbrellas to use, inflicting the wrath of the Lord on Wesley. Because of the repeated blows he still was unable to get his pants up. Each time he reached to pull them over his private parts, one of the ladies would smack him in such a way that he would fall back, enhancing the display the ladies found so despicable.

The last of the reporters departed, and patrons from

the gin shop next door started to notice the ruckus. The bravest, or the drunkest, ascended the steps, not without some difficulty. He poked his multicolored nose (mostly red but with streaks of blue and a touch of black soot on the very end) through the door the departing reporters had failed to close. “Lordy, dey is a-beating a peer naked feller. Comes an’ watch, now. Dey is a-gonna beats his balls offen ’im.” The crowd began gathering as people started staggering out of the gin shop. Pushing and shoving, hair pulling, and fist fighting was the natural result. That’s when the police arrived.

Chapter 60

While the Bobbies were breaking up the riot, while Percy Wesley was lying exposed on the floor still being pummeled by umbrellas, while the clergymen who had accompanied the matrons of the Vice Society were attending to the corpse of the costermonger, they did not want to notice how the ladies were relishing their abuse of the Queen's Minister of Public Safety. Forster provided large warm coats for the two professional women and ushered his troupe of actors down the back stairs. Then Barbary and his first cousin and his second cousin drove everyone back to the Black Lion. When they got to the door, the girls wouldn't go in. "'Taint our sorta place, ducky," Nell explained. Caddy Quale paid them generously for their work.

Forster told them, "Indeed, it was a wonderful performance. I may be calling on you ladies for a little show I am planning for the Drury. Thank you so much for your help." The women tucked their payment in the usual place, and Barbary's second cousin agreed to deliver them to their usual neighborhood. He apparently knew where it was without asking.

Inside, a jolly fire burned. Clara and Barkis, himself, served drinks, and a generous luncheon consisting of hot steak and kidney pie, bangers, mashed potatoes, and boiled parsnips sat on a long table in the taproom. Clara counted heads as the group tramped in. "No one has been injured, then. Where are the girls?"

Caddy said, "They didn't want to come in, but they are fine. Didn't they just want to get back to business, so to say. Faith, an' I have a feeling they didn't think they were properly dressed."

Barkis, himself, said, "That be a shame." Clara hit him with a wooden spoon.

Blathers was the first to have a drink, because the others had stopped to view the lunch table. "Savin' me country from them rats be thirsty work, ya knows." He downed a pint of dark ale and was back for a brandy long before I was able to find a spot of milk for my tea.

After everyone, including Barbary, and his first cousin, and his second cousin, who had returned from delivering the female members of the cast to their quarters, was made comfortable with beverages and stuffed with the wholesome food, each recounted his impression of the performance.

Forster started by declaring the play was a roaring success. "Of course, we shall have to wait for the reviews, which, thanks to Charles, should be in the afternoon papers."

"I certainly hope so," Dickens said. "Those lads certainly drink a great deal. I don't quite remember from my days as court reporter that there was that much liquor consumed."

"Come now, Charles," Forster responded, "You know the main reason they agreed to come along on your adventure was that you were supplying the liquor."

"I know, John. But I didn't plan on their drinking so much. It was good luck that Barbary's cousin had something in his cab to ward off the chill."

"I is 'is second cousin, as ya knows, and ya is very welcome."

Clara said, "You needn't worry about what each has contributed to the matter. The lady arranged for all to be repaid with a bonus. She paid for a lovely lunch and all the beverages. So drink up, Mr. Blathers."

Blathers was not being shy about his consumption. He was having a good old time, and he kept chuckling to himself. "The great scene were that little dandy there on the floor wi' his pants down round his ankles, and the ladies o' the Vice Society keeps knockin' him back down so's they can has another look at his"—Blathers remembered that Clara was present—"pre-dick-erment." Barbary's first and second cousins laughed. I think I blushed. Blathers said, "I'll has another wee drop o' brandy, if'n ya please, Mr. Barkis."

Barkis went to fetch more drinks. Barbary's cousins were making every effort to guarantee the cold and damp of the London streets would not trouble them. The door opened, and a voice said, "Da aternoon papers, Mr. Barkis."

Forster jumped from his chair and grabbed the papers just as any producer would do on opening night. He read the headlines aloud.

"Minister of Public Safety Involved in Murder"; "Vice Society Declares Minister an Abomination"; "The Iron Duke Disowns Cousin"; "Queen Sacks Minister"; "Public Safety Responsibility of Scotland Yard"; "Thugs Held for Three Murders."

A cheer went up; drinks were served all around. I added a drop of brandy to my tea. "Here's to Joe."

TALE THREE

Three Problems to Solve
Summer 1845

There is a villain dwelling in England.

Chapter One

We heard about the cryptic message just a month past. Then, some thugs attacked Blathers and me, and then, the same day, we heard about the murder.

Blathers and I are doing quite well as consulting detectives. We have made our headquarters at the Black Lion. No, not in the taproom. With the introduction of train travel, there are fewer overnight guests at the inn. It isn't close enough to any of the train depots now used by travelers. The sound of the Bristol Coach pulling into the yard of the venerable old establishment is a thing of the past.

The room we lease from Clara and Barkis, himself, previously used by travelers for overnight accommodations, is a first-floor front, with a view of the entrance to the inn. The slaughter of Lizabeth Stride happened in the room across the hall, back when Phil Squod owned the place. In truth, I am the one usually using the space, as Blathers does spend much of his time in the taproom. We have set up an office of sorts. We meet with our clients in the room, and I maintain some written files.

One amazing thing has happened. Blathers has decided he wants to learn to read, and I assume he will learn to write at the same time. Apparently he is interested in reading some of Mr. Dickens' work for himself. Everyone is talking about his novels, and Blathers, although he is personally acquainted with the celebrated writer, as am I, feels left out.

Since we have been partners for these many years, I thought it only natural I should teach him. But, at our first lesson we had a bit of a spat. There is no truth, however, to his accusation I called him a dunderhead. In any event, he has employed a young woman to give him lessons. He seems to relish his meetings with her.

****

It was just noon when I went downstairs for lunch. Blathers was there with his pint. He had already ordered his meal.

I said, "You're back from your lesson early today. I believe we were not expecting you until half one."

"Me teacher had an appointment this afternoon, didn't she. She was obliged ta end the lesson early."

"I see. And what kind of a woman is she?"

"She's a very neat lady and a patient teacher, which is more than I can say fer some."

"Ah, neat is she, and I wager quite young and attractive?"

"She's about ten or twelve years younger than you or me. As I says, she's neat, and pleasant, and well educated. She were, er, I mean was, a governess fer a very well-placed family, but she loosed, lost her position and come away wi'out any references."

"How did that happen? Was she caught stealing?"

"All she'll say is she lost her position but kept her honor, and that's the whole story. Now she has students like me. She teaches readin' and writin' and proper ways o' talkin', and she has some ladies what is new rich she teaches manners and how ta dress and all. She seems ta be doin' quite well fer herself."

Blathers was blushing slightly during this whole conversation, although his complexion was so naturally ruddy only I, since we have been partners for so long, was familiar enough with him to notice the darkening in color. He said, "If'n you're through wi' your questionin' now, ya can wipe the silly grin aff your face."

"One last question. What's her name, and when will I get to meet her?"

"Them's two questions."

"All right, two last questions then."

"Her name is Alice Martin, and…" At that moment the door opened, and I saw a very lovely woman of about five-and-twenty looking around the room. Clara Barkis hurried to greet her. "Would you care to be seated in the parlor, miss?"

"Uh, no, I'm looking for Mr. Blathers. I understand he can usually be found here."

On hearing his name, Blathers looked up from his pint and his cheese sandwich. When he saw the woman, he jumped to his feet, and I noticed the additional redness return to his face. "Miss Martin, I'm just havin' finished me lunch, but I'm sure Mrs. Barkis will be happy ta seat ya in the parlor if'n you're in need of a meal. I could join ya there, and ya can tells me, tell me, why ya has, er, why you have, called."

"I'm not at all hungry, Mr. Blathers, and I am quite comfortable in a taproom. My father was an innkeeper."

"Then please be seated," Clara said.

Alice accepted the chair the cordial hostess of the Black Lion placed at the table. I remained seated and waited for Blathers to introduce the lady. I knew it to be poor taste for a man to introduce himself to an unmarried lady. Alice Martin also waited for Blathers to do the proper thing. Nothing happened. Finally, I said, "Blathers, remember you etiquette."

"Me edicut?"

Alice laughed, and touched Blathers' arm lightly. "I am afraid, Mr. Blathers, that I do not know this gentleman."

"Oh, me edicut. Well, this here's no gentleman. This be me partner, Duff."

I stood and took the lady's hand, bowed, and said, "At your service, Miss Martin."

Blathers said, "Now the edicut is done, will ya has, have, a pint, Miss Martin?"

"I'll be damned if I won't," this from a most proper lady, "and then I'll tell you why I need a detective."

****

Jane served fresh pints of bitter to Miss Martin and Blathers. Clara served tea to me. She brought a pint of stout for herself. Barkis, himself, was off carting for the afternoon, which meant that Clara could partake freely of the potables available from the Black Lion's taps. "Isn't it lovely to have Jane back after all this time. We offered to give her back her evening position, but now she prefers the day work."

We were all happy to see Jane after her long absence caring for her ill aunt. She was still quite attractive, although slightly heavier than when she went away almost four years ago.

After a long drink from her pint, the very neat Miss Martin brought forth a wrinkled and worn piece of paper from her reticule. "My information is confidential, Mr. Blathers."

"Oh, ya can speak freely in front o' Duff. He's me longtime partner, and though he's a bit stuffy, you know, he's trustworthy as a oak tree. And our dear landlady, Clara Barkis, knows all we is doin' anyway. She says nary a word ta anyone."

I resented being called stuffy, but I wished to reassure the young lady. "You can be sure all you tell us will be held in confidence by all here, Miss Martin. We have provided services for the gentry and for government officials. They selected us because of our reputation for protecting secrets, and Clara has always been somewhat of an assistant in our cases."

Clara drank to that.

Miss Martin appeared to be satisfied and unfolded the paper. "I was surprised to see a Maltese cross on the sign in front of the inn, for, as you see, there is a Maltese cross embossed on the top of this paper."

Clara said, "Ah, that sign has been there for well over a hundred years. Me and Barkis had it repainted just as it was when we took over the place. We don't have any idea about it, except the lion is black. The rest of the stuff is just the stuff was there." The sign of the Black Lion was a lion couchant, bearing in his dexter paw a Maltese cross.

I said, "Well, I believe all of the items in a coat of arms indicate something. Perhaps a little research into heraldic symbolism is in order."

"Them is big words. Has ya been studyin' big words while I was studyin' wi' Miss Martin here?"

Miss Martin laughed. It seemed she really was enjoying the tutoring of Blathers. He was probably an eager learner, but no doubt there was a long way to go. She said, "The cross isn't the only mystery here. Look at the writing. It is very strange. None of it seems to make sense."

I took the paper and studied it. "Where did this come from?"

"My brother gave it to me when I visited him today. He is in the army and will be going out of the country soon. He entrusted this to me because he did not want to take it with him in the event he…perishes in battle. He only recently came into possession of the paper and has not had an opportunity to determine what it is. All he knows is that it is valuable."

"How does he know that?"

"A mortally wounded man in his regiment gave it to him. He swore on his deathbed it contained a secret that would provide untold riches. He gave the paper to my brother with the request that whatever wealth was discovered be used in a good cause. My brother said he was particularly interested in the plight of young men who have come from the country to London looking for work. He had done so himself, but he fell in with bad company and was arrested. That was how he ended up in the army."

I asked, "Are you sure this isn't Greek, or Latin, or some other foreign language?"

"I'm familiar with both Greek and Latin, and I am certain it is not either of those. It is the strangest concoction of letters I have ever seen."

I expressed a thought. "Perhaps it's a code of some type, the kind where one letter is substituted for another. That might account for the odd arrangement of the letters." It was clear our first problem was to discern the meaning of the cryptic note. "May I suggest, Miss Martin, that we adjourn upstairs to our office. I would like to make a copy of your letter so I can attempt to solve the code."

Blathers apparently felt we needed a chaperon, because he jumped up and said, "I'll be goin' along wi' ya." He had not finished his pint.

Clara suggested that Blathers and the young lady take their beverages with them, and the three of us ascended the slanted and rickety stairway to our room. Clara returned to the tap and topped off her stout.

Chapter Two

"I'll be wantin' ta make a copy o' the letter too," Blathers announced.

"What for? You can't read yet, can you?"

"I can read some, can't I, Miss Martin. Besides, even a smart feller like you, who's had all the learning and such, can't read what's written here."

"You're correct there. I'm sorry. I'll make two copies, and we can both try to decode it." I wrote down the following on two sheets of fresh paper I took from a wooden box on top of the worktable.

RERBRJ DONLBK ZESPCL SQUODA
IFIJEB VJGFKC DPRQGD WIRXVE
ZXYJIF ZUSKHG FAOLVH ZLMZ~ I

"Well, this is very strange indeed. I hardly know where to start," I said.

"My brother has had some experience in cryptography while in the army. Unfortunately, he had no opportunity to work on the message before he had to leave with his regiment. He did say one thing, though. He noticed the letters were arranged six to a group. He said this was unusual. Letters are usually arranged five to a group in coded messages. He has never seen anyone use six-letter sequences."

Blathers scratched the back of his neck and stared at the message. "I does notice one thing."

"You do notice one thing, Mr. Blathers."

"I does, yes."

"No, no, you do. You do."

"Ah, yes, I do notice one thing. Thank ya, Miss Martin. If'n ya only use five letters instead o' six, I do notice Squod's name at the end o' the first line."

Alice said, "Squod? Who is Squod?"

I explained. "He was the landlord of the Black Lion before Mr. and Mrs. Barkis took the place over. There was a murder here, and Blathers and I suspected Squod's son, Jack. We came here to question him, and he ran. Nary a soul has heard of him since. Squod was a drunk, and after the murder, and Jack's disappearance, he was unable to run the business."

Alice shook her head. "And now Squod's name appears in a coded message, and there is a Maltese cross on the message, and there is a Maltese cross on the sign over the door."

Chapter Three

Blathers said, “I sees your pint be empty, Miss Martin.”

“I see your pint is empty.”

“Yes, it is too.”

“No, no! You should say, I see your pint is empty. Remember, you must make the verb agree with the noun. You remember that, don’t you?”

“Oh, yes! I see your pint is empty, Miss Martin.”

“Much better, but I think you and Mr. Duff should get used to calling me Alice. And I would like to call you by your first names, but I don’t know what they are.”

Blathers looked at me. I shook my head and explained to Alice, “We don’t use first names. There is a reason, but we won’t go into that now. Just call us Blathers or Duff. Never mind the Mister part.”

“Well, I’ll respect that, but you will call me Alice. I insist.”

Blathers said carefully, “Well, Alice, both of our pints are still empty.”

“That they are, Blathers. Shall we go down to the taproom?”

Alice took Blathers’ arm and started toward the crooked stairway. “Will you be joining us, Duff?”

“I’ll be along in a bit. I wish to spend a little time

to see if I can make anything out of this cipher. Be careful on the stairs. They are quite old and not at all straight. There may be a loose board or two, so watch your step."

****

Once Alice and Blathers were off to imbibe, I was able to concentrate on the puzzle before me. I have some limited experience working with codes, from the time Blathers and I were detectives with the Bow Street Runners. That was before our short time with the Metropolitan Police. Back in '29, Sir Robert Peel melded the Runners into the Metropolitan Police. Blathers and I tried it for a while, but we couldn't get used to the formal ways of a modern police department.

Based on my experience, I agreed with Alice's brother about it being traditional to separate messages into units of five letters. This avoids the use of word length as an aid to breaking the code. In this case there were six letters, except for the last word, where a dash appeared. I thought maybe this wasn't a substitution code at all.

I recalled there was another type of code where groups of letters arranged in some geometric form would reveal the message. I tried the most obvious and came up with nothing.

I did notice the last letters in each group were in sequence J K L A B C D E F G H I. Perhaps the last letter was some kind of indicator. I tried several possibilities, adjusting the sequence and geometric form. Still nothing.

I decided to make a list of the things I knew about the cipher. This would help me to think logically and would, I hoped, point to some other ways to decode the message. As I withdrew another sheet of paper from the box on my desk, I heard a ruckus in the taproom. At least it sounded like a ruckus to me. To Blathers and Alice and Clara, it sounded like singing.

Chapter Four

I thought that I had best look in on the trio in the taproom. I suspected that if Barkis, himself, came home from his carting job and found Clara in a less than stable condition, he might be upset. Then life around the Black Lion would be tense for several days. Barkis is an easygoing man, but he is concerned about Clara's tendency to indulge. Blathers quite often is a source of temptation for her. I certainly would not like to see our landlord upset to the extent he would terminate our tenancy at the inn. Now I hoped Alice was not going to turn out to be someone who added to the problem. Based on the singing, I was sure it was a good thing Jane was back on duty.

I hurried down the narrow stairway. There was a board on one step that was more warped, worn, and wiggly than the others. As I stepped on it, it moved, and I lost my balance. The only thing that kept me from tumbling down the remaining stairs was the narrowness of the stairwell itself. I bounced off the opposite wall and landed in a most ungainly position on the next step. The plank that caused my fall tore loose. Being a man of action and being unwilling to have the others find me in this situation, I removed my shoe and pounded the plank back into position. I then rose from the floor, dusted off my breeches, and proceeded to the taproom.

"I wonder if any of you are in any condition to assist me in getting to the bottom of this coded message."

The three faces, all a little flushed by this time, stared at me. Blathers said, "We was just about ta come up and see if we could a helped ya, but then we hears this great racket on the stairs, and we thinks ya must has been drinkin' sompthin' up there yourself."

Alice said, "That we was." She put down her glass. "But I think I should go home now. Blathers, will you see me to a hansom?"

Clara said, "I must see to the preparations for dinner."

They left me alone in the taproom without even a cup of tea.

I shrugged and called to Clara, who was now banging pots and pans in the kitchen. "Clara, if you have a hammer, I'll finish the repair to the stair."

"Here's the hammer, and here's some nails. Hammer it down good so there are no further accidents."

"Give me all the nails. There are several other planks coming loose. I'll nail them down, as well." Sometimes, banging away with a hammer is a good way to overcome frustration.

Chapter Five

There was nothing to do after my hammering but return upstairs and prepare my list. As I turned to go, the taproom door swung open, and a quite well-dressed man entered.

"I say, you! I'm looking for a young woman, Alice Martin. Do you know her, old chap?"

He seemed to be a well-to-do, jovial old fellow, quite harmless.

"May I inquire as to your interest in Miss Martin?"

"Careful fellow, aren't you. Good chap! Can't be too careful these days. Say, how about a drink, on me, of course. Hum, no one here." He bellowed, "Who's in the bar?" and rapped on a table with his umbrella. Jane came from the kitchen swinging her hips, much to the delight of the old gentleman.

"A brandy for me and whatever this fellow drinks."

"Oh, he only drinks tea, sir."

"Whatever. Only drink tea, do you? Some medical condition, no doubt. Poor fellow. Well, enjoy your tea. Make that a double brandy for me, if you please, young lady."

The gentleman turned to me and said, "Sit, sit. Enjoy your tea." He extended his hand. "Name's Childers, Harold Childers. Miss Martin was in the employ of my household. I have just discovered we have done her a great injustice."

The taproom door flew open once again, and a young dandy rushed in. "Father, what are you doing? This thing is none of your business. Please don't interfere. This is between Alice and me."

"Ah, Mister, er, what is your name, old chap?"

"My name is Duff, Mr. Childers."

"Yes, yes, Duff! Mr. Duff, this is my son, Edward Childers. I am sorry to say that he is the cause of the injustice of which I speak."

As Childers was introducing me, Blathers returned to the room. The fresh air must have helped him clear his head. He was no longer singing, just humming.

"Ah, Blathers, these gentlemen are here looking for Miss Martin. This is Mr. Childers and his son. They are Miss Martin's previous employers."

Blathers asked, "What do ya want wi' her? What makes ya think she is here? I doesn't think she would care ta sees ya."

Mr. Childers Senior responded, "Now, now, my good man, easy. I found out this morning that I had made a mistake when I released the young lady from her position. I went to her lodgings to make amends, but she was not home. The landlady said she might have left with a Mr. Blathers who maintained a business location at the Black Lion Inn. I see I have found Mr. Blathers. Can you tell me where to find Miss Martin?"

Blathers turned to the younger Childers. "What about you?"

"I followed my father. Once again he has misunderstood the situation and is acting irrationally. Father, we must talk before you go further with this matter. You are not aware of all of the facts. You always go running off before anyone can explain anything to you."

"Now you listen to me, lad. I didn't just appear on this earth at the age of forty-five, you know. I was young once. I have had some experience. I'll take care of everything."

The elder Mr. Childers poured down his brandy, grabbed his hat off the chair, and departed without another word.

Chapter Six

Edward Childers slumped into the chair his father had vacated. "He never listens. He always goes off like a faulty pistol, just as spontaneous and just as deadly."

Blathers pulled a chair up to the table and joined the young man and me. Blathers said, "Will ya has a brandy, young feller?"

"Why, yes, I need something."

Seeing that Jane was busy in the kitchen, Blathers went behind the bar and brought out two glasses and the brandy bottle. He poured a drink for Edward and one for himself. I hoped he wouldn't start to sing again. He said, "Now, young feller, would ya like ta tell us all about it?" It seemed the beverages were helping Blathers observe the rules of grammar a little better. I wondered if he and Miss Martin drank during their lessons.

Edward began his story. "I'm not sure what has happened. Alice came to work for us as a teacher for my younger brothers and sister. I was taken with her. And I believed at the time she liked me.

"One afternoon, we happened to meet in the hallway in front of the door to my father's study. We were embracing when we heard my mother's voice from the drawing room. We quickly tried the door to the study, and, finding it unlocked, ducked inside. We thought we were safe, as we believed my father was not in the house. We were mistaken, for within a few minutes my father entered the room and found us there. He, as usual, overreacted. He dismissed Alice, Miss Martin, on the spot, telling her to pack and leave the premises immediately. He banished me to my rooms just as though I were a child. All the time he kept yelling, 'You all know the rule is that no one is allowed in my study.' When mother came to see what the commotion was, he physically pushed her out of the room and slammed the door."

I said, "He sounds like a man with a quick temper."

Blathers added, "Yes, and very protective of his room."

"You have seen what he is like here this afternoon. This morning when we talked and he discovered I was still seeing Alice, and that I had become best of friends with her brother, he exploded again. In a complete turn around he declared he had mistreated her, and when I told him she was doing quite well giving instructions to private students in the front room of her flat on The Strand, he went raging out of the house to find her. That is how we have come to be here.

"I must go now to see if I can find her before some other crazy thing happens."

Blathers jumped to his feet. "I think I'll go along wi' you. She has asked me and Duff fer our help. She may needs it if'n you and your father is both at her at the same time."

Young Childers and Blathers left to go to Miss Martin's flat. I went back to our room to work on the coded message. I returned, once again, to my idea of making a list of all the facts I had already discovered about the code. After a short while I had the following:

1.Substitution ciphers are traditionally divided into groups of five letters. This one has six letters in each group, except the last. The fifth letter is a dash.

2. The final letters of each group are consecutive from A to L. But the A to L sequence starts with the fourth word.

3. If "A", the sixth letter, is dropped from the fourth word, the name of the former owner of the Black Lion is spelled out.

4. There is a Maltese cross embossed on the paper containing the original message. There is a Maltese cross on the sign of the Black Lion.

5. It appears that rearranging the order of either the letters or the units of letters cannot solve the cipher.

Looking at the list, I was surprised to find I actually knew this much. On the other hand, I was surprised to find that, at this point, I was not able to go further. I studied my list. I studied the cipher. I studied the ceiling of our room. Nothing!

I thought that sometimes it is helpful to set a project of this nature aside. As it was nearing the end of the day, I locked my copy of the cipher and my attempts at decoding in a strong box where Blathers and I keep cash, papers, and other valuables, and set out for home. Before leaving the inn, I peeked into the taproom to see if Blathers had returned. He had not.

In the street, a thick fog had descended, bringing down with it all of the smoke of a thousand home fires. Every avenue, alley, and doorway was full of the foul-smelling, soaking-wet air. If I extended my arm out in front of me, I could not see my fingertips.

The poor visibility meant little to me. I was very

used to my way of returning home. A few steps from the door of the inn I found the alley that would lead to The Strand. I was just into the alley when I heard a strange sound behind me. That is the last I remember.

Chapter Seven

When I came to, I was wet throughout from the fog. I was lying propped up against the wall of a building. My assailant had turned out my pockets. The contents—two one-pound notes, several coins, and a pocket watch given to me by my father upon the occasion of my confirmation in the established church—lay in my lap. Nothing was missing, but I was wet and chilled, and I had a severe headache.

Because of the weather, there were no other persons about to aid me, so I picked myself up and got myself home. There I stripped in front of the fire and heated water for a bath. After taking some headache powders, which I always have on hand, I settled in and slept the night away.

****

The next morning, when I arrived at the Black Lion, I imposed on Clara for an extra strong cup of tea. "It was quite a severe blow, my dear Clara, but I am surviving. Your lovely tea will help."

"You were robbed in the fog, then, Mr. Duff?"

"It wasn't a robbery, as nothing was taken. If it was a thief, at least the pound notes and the watch would have been gone. I cannot fathom the reason for the assault. By the way, have you seen Blathers since he left yesterday afternoon with the young lad?"

"He hasn't been here. He usually stops in the evening for a drop before retiring to his digs, but last night he never appeared."

After a second cup and a trip to the back yard of the inn, I went up to the office and again tried to concentrate on the puzzling message. Because of the throbbing in my head, I found it difficult to focus on my work. There was also something else troubling me. Blathers was missing. I kept leaving my table and wandering to the window, in case I could see him approaching on the street. He was usually late in arriving, and he would often stop in the bar and join Clara in what they called their "eye opener." But he had never been this late. It was raining, but the fog had lifted from the city, even though it had not lifted from my head. There seemed to be no excuse for his not arriving.

Shortly before noon, I could stand it no longer. Back in the taproom I asked, "Has there been any sign of Blathers or any message from him, Clara? Today is not a day for his lesson, is it?"

"No, he went yesterday, and he is not again scheduled until day after tomorrow. There has been nary a sign nor a sound of him. If he isn't here in the next few minutes, then we should really worry. It's his lunchtime."

"I agree. If he isn't hungry, he is thirsty, for certain. The last we knew, he was off to Miss Martin's rooms. Do you have any idea where she is located?"

"I know she is on The Strand, somewhat near Blathers' place. He has often said it was only a short distance from his rooms to his lessons. That's why he usually would go there first thing in the morning."

"Perhaps I'll walk down that way and see what I can see. If he comes in, ask him to wait until I return."

I picked up my umbrella and pulled the door open. As I did so, Blathers came in. He was soaked through and looked worse than I felt. "Where have you been, and what has happened to you?"

Blathers shuffled to one of the chairs, plopped down, and said, "Clara, a double brandy, if'n ya please."

Clara recognized the dire need and brought the double brandy without saying a word. Blathers took an unusually long drink, swallowed, took another, looked at me, and said in perfectly correct English, "Miss Martin's brother has been murdered."

Chapter Eight

Blathers moved to a chair in front of the fire to dry while he explained the situation. “When young Childers and I got ta Alice’s flat, there were a army officer there. Alice were in tears. The officer told us he were there ta report that Major Martin were discovered stabbed ta death in his rooms. When the major didn’t arrive ta meet his regiment at the proper time, they sent this young feller to find him. When he discovered the body, he sent fer his captain, and they sent fer the Peelers.”

Clara said, “Ah, the poor girl. Is someone with her in her grief?”

“I believes she is alone now. The army man told me where the major’s digs was, so I left the Childers lad with her and went off ta investigate fer meself. When I got ta the scene, them Bobbies was everywhere. They wouldn’t talk wi’ me, of course. Ya knows how they is, don’t ya, Duff. One did say the landlady were quite upset and had run off ta the local fer some liquid courage.

“I found her there wi’ a large gin, and it weren’t her first. When I bought her a third, she was able ta finally get herself together enough ta tell me what happened.”

The landlady had told Blathers that, soon after Miss Martin left her brother’s place, two men called on the major. She said the way they were dressed made her think they were government officials. They stayed nearly an hour, and then about another hour after they left, the young army officer arrived, looking for Major Martin. When he didn't answer his door, the landlady let the officer in and they discovered the body. The hoodlums had ransacked the rooms.

"It were quite late when I finally offered ta help the landlady back ta her digs. By that time the fog were thick as can be, and I may have had an extra pint meself. Anyway, I was finding me way in the fog when I sees these two shadows comin' at me way wi' what looks like clubs in their hands. All of a sudden one takes a swipe at me head. Good show there were a lamppost there that the feller didn't notice. The club bounced off the lamppost instead o' me. Well, we, er, I ducks into a doorway, pulls out me pistol, and fires in the direction o' the two shadows. I hears one let out a yelp, and that's the last I sees o' them."

Clara asked again, "Have you been to see Miss Martin this morning, then?"

"No, I is just getting out o' the house now. It were very late when I gets home, you know. It took some time ta gets the full story from the landlady, and she were afraid ta go back ta her place. I needed ta help her find a place ta stay fer the night."

No one asked Blathers any further questions about his investigation. I did notice that, when Alice was not present, Blathers cared less about the correct use of the language. Perhaps he was just excited and forgot what he had learned.

I told Blathers about the assault on me. Clara said, "You mean that Major Martin has been murdered, you,

Duff, have been knocked unconscious, you, Blathers, had to fend off attackers with gunshots, and you have left poor dear Miss Martin alone?”

Chapter Nine

Blathers and I rushed through the alley to The Strand and hurried toward Alice Martin's flat. The rain had stopped, but we each carried an umbrella against the certainty the downpour would start again soon. It was quicker to walk than it would be to get a cab. Blathers found rushing difficult, so I arrived at our destination several minutes sooner than he did. I knew I had reached Alice's flat because a Bobbie stood in front of her door. I stopped and caught my breath, relieved that our haste was unnecessary. While I rested, Blathers caught up.

"Well, look here. Guardin' the door o' our lovely Alice is our favorite Bobbie of all time, Young Jerry Cruncher. How is ya, Young Jerry? Has ya been out here in the fog and rain all the night and day?"

"Go'day, Mr. Blathers. Go'day, Mr. Duff. No, I 'asn't been 'ere all the night. I'm a senior man now, and I no longer needs ta work nights. Them newer fellers do that, donch ya see. I come on at 'alf eight. The feller what were 'ere all the night in the fog were quite wet, 'e were. I 'as me raincoat, donch ya see."

I told Young Jerry we were here to see Miss Martin. He confirmed that, because of the brutality of the attack on her brother, his superiors had assigned him and his fellow officers to guard the young woman.

"I can lets ya go in, but I 'as ta go wi' ya, donch ya know." We three trooped to Alice's main floor door. "These gents is 'ere ta sees ya, miss. Does ya wants me ta shoo them away?"

"Oh, no, no, Constable. Please let them come in. Thank you for coming, Mr. Blathers, Mr. Duff. Thank you so much. Please, please, come in."

Cruncher started to enter the house with us, but Blathers looked at him so fiercely he stepped back and returned to the street without saying a word.

Inside, Blathers said, "Dear Alice, Duff and I are so very sorry about the loss of your brother, and we are concerned about your being here alone. Clara has asked us to extend an invitation for you to stay at the Black Lion, as her guest, for as long as you like. We would be very pleased if you would pack what things you need and come along with us now. We all feel that you will be much happier and safer if you accept her invitation."

I was flabbergasted. Blathers had talked like his old self, all morning. I guessed it was because he had been excited, but now, in the presence of Alice, he was even using the possessive with the participle. I could say nothing to either of them. I just nodded in agreement. Alice must have noticed the eloquence of the speech as well, for, in spite of her grief, a smile formed on her lovely lips.

"I am sure being with you and Mrs. Barkis will be right for me. Please give me a few minutes to put some things together."

Blathers, still in his Queen's English mode, said, "I will go and speak to Cruncher, and arrange for a cab."

Since Miss Martin didn't need my help packing, I went out with Blathers. I had witnessed discussions between my partner and the young constable, and I found them amusing. I didn't want to miss this exchange.

"Young Jerry, there, be a good lad and keep an eye out fer a cab, will ya? We is taking Miss Martin wi' us as soon as she is ready." Apparently this conversation did not require any eloquence.

"Takin'? Where is ya takin' 'er? I can't lets ya take 'er anywhere. I is guardin' 'er, donch ya see."

"Ya was guardin' her, but now we is guardin' her, and ya can go and has a cuppa."

"I can't do that. I 'as me orders, donch ya know."

Alice came to the street with her portmanteau as Jerry was waving his hands in the air, and Blathers had his right index finger placed squarely on the Peeler's breastplate.

"You're not holding the lady a prisoner. That is against the law, and unless you are going to arrest her you cannot detain her." Blathers was becoming a language chameleon, changing the color of his speech depending on the circumstances, the circumstance in this case being the presence of Alice Martin.

"I 'as me orders. I can't let ya takes the lady. I 'as ta talk to me gov 'bout it."

"Jerry, my friend, we do not have time to wait for your superior to come along. Now, let us think about this."

"Is ya all right, Mr. Blathers? Ya sounds very strange."

"Never mind, now, my lad, how I sound. Just answer me this one question. What exactly were your orders?"

"I 'as told ya, me orders is ta guard the lady."

"Exactly. You are to guard the lady, not the house. Here, Duff, grab that cab and the one behind it. Up you go, Alice. Duff, I'll ride with Alice. You and Jerry take the second cab. He can guard her at the Lion."

Chapter Ten

Alice and Clara gathered around one of the tables in the taproom with me and Blathers. Alice and I had tea. As usual, Blathers and Clara had their hands wrapped around pint glasses. We were discussing our adventures of the day before. The ancient oak door to the taproom creaked, and Clara's head snapped up. She slid her pint in front of me and pulled my mug of tea in front of her. Barkis, himself, entered the room. Clara said, "Ah, darling, I wasn't sure when to expect your return."

Barkis was usually a docile soul, in the background of every act, like a fireside stool. Today was different. "Me cart broke down in the worst of the rain. The goods were soaked, and the consignee would not accept delivery. I told him the carter weren't responsible fer acts o' God, and if the goods was subject ta damage cause o' rain then they should ha been packed 'cordingly. He makes me take ever'thin' back ta the shipper, and I won't get paid fer that."

"Sit down, dear, and let me get you something to eat. I have a lovely shepherd's pie."

"I isn't hungry. What's that Bobbie doin' standing in front o' the door? That can't be good fer business. No customers is gonna tell the Bobbie ta move so's they can come in. And has ya been at the taps again,

Clara, or has Duff taken ta drinking ale, now?"

I didn't know what to say, but Blathers always seems to be able to concoct a story to ease a difficult situation. "Ah, now, Barkis, take it easy. Duff has had a rough few days. He were, was coshed last night, and he has a bad head this morning. He thought he would try a spot of ale to see if it would help, didn't you, Duff?"

"I did, but I don't like it. I don't think I'll finish it."

"Never you mind, I will drink it for you." Blathers poured the remains of what was Clara's pint into his own mug. "And I will take care of the Bobbie for you, as well, Barkis." He got out of his chair and went to the front door.

Very shortly he returned. "Young Jerry has decided that his gov will be looking for him, and, as long as we are with Miss Martin, he'll return to headquarters and get new instructions. You see, Barkis, how simple these things are."

Barkis went to the tap and drew himself a pint. "I guess you're right. I needs ta relax. Will ya have a pint as well, Clara? One won't hurt ya. And I'll has some o' that shepherd's pie now, if ya please. What has ya folks been talkin 'bout? I'll just sits down here and join ya."

Clara said, "I will have a pint. This is Miss Alice Martin, the poor dear. Someone has murdered her brother. She is going to stay with us for a while."

"Go'day, Miss Martin. Please accept me sympathies fer the loss o' your brother. Ya is welcome ta be our guest fer as long as necessary." Barkis had resumed his natural personality.

I explained the highlights of our situation to him and finished by saying, "I think our first problem is to solve the cryptic message."

"That can't be too hard. There be only twenty-six possibilities, if'n it be one o' them substitution things, ya know. There's five o' us. We ought ta be able ta figure it out right quick."

Alice agreed. "Yes, we can all help. Can't we, Mr. Blathers?" She had noticed the look on Blathers face. "It is simply knowing your alphabet. Isn't that correct, Mr. Barkis?"

Barkis nodded, and I went to our room to get my copy of the coded message and some more paper and pens and ink. We would have a comfortable afternoon, and at the end of our exercise we should have the answer we sought.

Chapter Eleven

Several patrons had come in for their noon meal, lured either by the scent of shepherd's pie or by draft ale. Blathers and Alice each decided they also wished to have a serving of Clara's delicious dish. I was still not feeling quite well, so Jane served toasted brown bread and marmalade for me. As soon as Jane had cleared all the tables from lunch, and the taproom patrons had returned to their daily tasks, we settled in to work on our puzzle.

Alice seemed distracted. "Do you think if we decipher the code it will help us discover who killed my brother? I would rather resolve that question than find untold riches."

I said, "I am quite sure your brother's murder, the assaults on Blathers and me, and the message are all connected. The cipher should help in discovering who our enemy is."

In addition to the coded message, I provided my list of things I had discovered about the cipher. The other members of our group were, quite naturally, impressed. Barkis wrote out a copy of the coded message and my list and went off to a small table by himself. He sat there studying both papers, and the back wall of the taproom. The rest of us huddled together at the large table, squirmed in our chairs, scratched the backs of our necks, stared at the ceiling, shuffled our feet, and occasionally said, "Hum!"

The old oak door creaked open again. "I say, you chaps look quite cozy, all tucked in this lovely bar. What do you have here? Looks like a sort of game. By Jove, I believe I'll join you. Madam, I'll have a double brandy, if you please." Harold Childers made himself comfortable by the fireplace.

Chapter Twelve

Blathers took charge again. "We were," he glanced at Alice, "just finishing up here, Mr. Childers. Make yourself comfortable while I collect the bits and pieces of our game." He quickly gathered the papers and carried them out of the room. Alice and Clara moved the pens and ink to a table near the wall.

Barkis, himself, looked confused. He was not aware of the sensitivity of the cipher. He scratched his head and said, "I just has had a thought." He scratched some more and looked around the room. "Well, I guesses it'll wait."

I asked, "What brings you out today, Mr. Childers?"

"Well, by Jove, I am looking for my son. There is an important business meeting today, new railroad, you know. The lad should be there. Good opportunity, don't you think? Say, you chaps wouldn't be interested in making an investment, would you? Railroads are the future, you know. Good chance to get on board, as they say." Childers chuckled, but his lips remained stiff, particularly the upper one. It seemed he was fearful of wrinkling his moustache.

I told him we had not seen the young man that day. "I believe that Blathers was with him yesterday." I remembered that Blathers had spent some time last evening, shall we say, being kind to Major Martin's landlady. I suspected the kindness spilled over to this morning, and that was the reason for his not arriving at his usual time.

Blathers said, "I haven't seen him since yesterday."

Barkis was agitated. "I see your glass is empty there, sir. Does ya wants another, or is ya goin' ta move on and look fer the lad?" Barkis grabbed the tumbler from Childers' hand.

Childers looked at the pens and inkbottles stacked on the side table. "Well, by Jove, since the game appears to be over, perhaps I will continue on my quest. What do I owe you for the brandy, landlord?"

Barkis was really anxious to have the man leave. "The drink is compliments o' the Black Lion, sir. Please ta come again."

The oak door was hardly closed when Barkis said, "I thinks I has some things that might help ta answer the cipher. I'll be back in a few minutes. Clara, where is the stuff I brung back from the army?"

"In the chest at the end of the bed."

Barkis hurried from the room.

Chapter Thirteen

There was a bit of uneasiness in the taproom. I wondered what our worthy host was up to. Blathers was rolling his eyes and scratching the back of his neck. Alice was wrinkling her brow as if to ask what was going on, and Clara seemed to be hoping that Barkis, himself, would not make a fool of himself. In the back of the building, where Clara and Barkis maintained their personal quarters, there were the sounds of banging and what might have been some swearing. Finally, we heard, "Ah! Here it is."

It was only a matter of seconds before Barkis appeared in the doorway with a diary or notebook of some kind and a small bronze disc. "I found them. This here's a cipher disc I brought from the war as a souvenir. I were sick o' killin', so's I didn't want no knives or guns or that sort. This here book and the disc belonged ta me mate what were part of the spies at one time. I'll show how it works. There's a few pages on decipherin' things. I thinks I can make use o' these on this here cipher."

Barkis pulled a chair up to the table where the rest of the party was gathered. There was a sense of awe among most of the group, although Clara seemed to still have some feeling of apprehension. "Now, love, are you sure you know what you're doing?"

"I feels quite sure I can make sense out o' this. First, let's see what the book says 'bout decodin', and then we should look at the things Mr. Duff has listed, the things he has found strange." I produced another copy of my analysis. "Then we'll use the disc."

Barkis took charge of the analysis. "Says here one thing we can do is—what's that word, Mr. Duff?" Barkis pointed to the book.

"Frequency."

"Right, frequency analyzin'. We counts the number o' each letter, and then we arranges them 'cordin' to how letters appear in the English language. Like it says here, "e" is the most frequent letter."

Alice said, "Well, let's give it a try. Lets each count the letters and see if we can spot the most frequent one." Everyone counted the letters separately.

Clara finally said, "How many letters are there in all?"

Alice answered, "Seventy-one and a dash. The dash must mean something."

Clara began to count again. "I only have sixty-eight."

Blathers said, "I have sixty-five," and began his recount.

At last everyone agreed on the count of seventy-one. "This don't make any sense." Barkis studied the results of the count. "The most of any letter is five and that happens four times. Next is four letters and that happens four times, as well. That's half the letters. It don't look—what's the word, Mr. Duff?"

"Frequency."

"That's it. It don't look like there be any frequency ta make note o'."

Clara said, "Oh! I'm sorry, dear. Let's try to figure out another approach with Mr. Duff's list. He makes the most lovely lists, doesn't he?"

Barkis balked. "How 'bout this here decodin' wheel? Let's give it a try. Says here in the book that it works ta help find the message when one letter is substituted fer 'nother."

I asked, "May I see your wheel, Mr. Barkis?"

The device was two different size circles of bronze connected on a hub at the center. The bottom disc was larger. The one on the top rotated on the center hub. Each disc had the alphabet imprinted on it. "Here's what we does, ya see. We figures that one letter in the code is equal ta 'A', and we sets the letter 'A' on the small disc to that letter. What letter does ya want ta try first?"

"Why, 'C' for Clara, my dear."

"Then we'll do 'C', and ta keep us from bein' confused, we'll use large letters for the code and small letters ta show our answer. So, if 'C' is equal to 'a,' what we does is set the decoder so that 'a' on the small disc is below 'C' on the large disc."

Barkis started writing letters on a sheet of my paper. When he finished, we looked at the results.

pcpzph bmljzi xcqnaj qosmby
gdghcz thedia bnpoeb ugpvtc
xvwhgd xsqife dymjtf xjkx~g

I took the wheel and checked Barkis' work. He was correct.

"But, dear, this doesn't make any sense. Are you sure this is the way this little thing works?"

I said, "Don't worry, Clara, I am quite certain Barkis is correct. We simply need to try other letters.

Let's try 'B' for Barkis. 'B' is equal to 'a'." Again I checked and verified the results. Again we were disappointed.

Blathers scratched the back of his neck. "If we do 'B' for Blathers, I think we'll get the same answer." He said all this without a grammatical error. "And if we use 'A' for Alice we don't get nothing different."

"Using 'A' for Alice won't give us anything different, Mr. Blathers."

"That's correct. If we end up with nothing, we won't have anything."

Alice said not a thing.

Blathers went on, "So, we have answers for 'A', 'B', and 'C'. We should try 'D' for Duff."

"D" for Duff produced nothing:

Alice said, "Only twenty-two more letters to go."

Blathers was getting impatient. "We can go along like this all afternoon and not get the answer."

I agreed, at least this one time, with my partner. "I think just finding the right letter to start on is too simple. The code has to be more complicated than that. We're missing something."

Alice asked, "Do you think the fact the message is arranged in units of six letters in lieu of five is a clue?"

"I am not sure. Let's look at my list again."

Chapter Fourteen

Several copies of the list were made, and one was given to each of the occupants of the taproom. Each studied his or her copy, which I reproduce here again for the convenience of the reader:

1. Substitution ciphers are traditionally divided into groups of five letters. This one has six letters in each group, except the last. The fifth letter is a dash.

2. The final letters of each group are consecutive from A to L. But the A to L sequence starts with the fourth word.

3. If the A, the sixth letter, is dropped from the fourth word, the name of the former owner of the Black Lion is spelled out.

4. There is a Maltese cross embossed on the paper containing the original message. There is a Maltese cross on the sign of the Black Lion.

5. It appears that rearranging the order of either the letters or the units of letters cannot solve the cipher.

Alice sat with her head down, looking at the paper in front of her, but she didn't seem to be reading or thinking about the items I had carefully defined. Then I noticed a tear run down her cheek. I asked, "What is it, Alice?"

"I don't see how any of this is going to help find the ones who killed my brother. All the time we fool with this silly puzzle, the killers are getting farther away." The brave face she had displayed up until now melted in a torrent.

Blathers was first on his feet, about to put his arms around the grieving girl, but as he neared her, he hesitated and stepped back, crossing his arms over his chest. Clara rose from her chair, without any difficulty, and hugged her, letting the tears dampen her comforting bosom. Everyone waited until the sobbing subsided.

"I'm sorry. It hurts so much. I'm trying to be brave, but it isn't easy."

"Now, now, my dear, you just let it out and don't worry about a thing. We are all friends here, and we all know how you must feel. Why don't I take you to your room, and you can have a little lie-down." Clara took Alice by the arm and helped her toward the stairway.

Barkis said, "Be careful on them stairs; they're always comin' loose."

With the ladies gone, I thought it might be wise to respond to Alice's despondent question. "You all may wonder if we are wasting our time with the coded message. Let me explain my thinking. I believe the people who killed Major Martin were looking for this document. The attacks on both Blathers and me support the theory. I also think the actual killers were hired thugs. It won't do us any good to spend time tracking them. The person or persons we want are the ones who hired the thugs. This message will help us to identify the real perpetrators."

Blathers said, "Okay, then lets be a-lookin' at this here list o' yours and sees if it can help us or not." Alice was out of the room. Blathers was out of his proper pronunciation.

Blathers scratched the back of his neck some more. Barkis stroked his chin. I tried to recall if the items on the list meant anything to me when I originally wrote them down. Nobody spoke for some moments, and soon Clara returned to the taproom. “I think she may nap a bit. Now, where are we on the message? Has there been any more thoughts?”

It was then we heard the stairs creak.

Chapter Fifteen

Alice stood in the taproom doorway. "I have an idea."

"Now, my dear, why don't you just go back up those stairs an' hop into bed."

"No, no, I have an idea about the message. Give me some paper and a pen." While Barkis gathered the supplies, Alice looked at the earlier attempts at solving by substitution.

She then said, "Now, you see, since the custom is to arrange letters in a group of five, I eliminate the last letter of each group. Now if I take the first five letters from the sequence of six that ends in 'a' I get 'squod.' That means something to us, does it not?"

We all agreed it did.

"Now let's do the same thing with the sequence that ends in 'b.' and 'c,' and 'd.' We get 'hehidthediamond' or, adding the 'a' letters, 'squodhehidthediamond.' Do you see it? 'squod he hid the diamond.' That tells me that the sixth letter is the answer. There is a different substitution for each group of five. In the first word, 'J' equals 'a', and in the second 'K' equals 'a', and so on. Go ahead and solve the puzzle."

Barkis had the substitution disc and went to work immediately. "I have it. The message is 'i visited brother squod he hid the diamonds entrusted to me by the order.' That leaves us with two new questions."

I said, "Yes! Who, or what is the 'order'?"

Blathers said, "Yes! And where are the diamonds?"

One puzzle solved; two new ones created.

The taproom door opened again.

Chapter Sixteen

"Me gov says I should come back 'ere and stays wi' the miss." Young Jerry Cruncher, head down in his shoulders, apparently scared Blathers would attack him, peeked into the room.

"Come in, Jerry my boy, and sit down." Blathers tried to soothe Cruncher's anxiety. I wanted to warn the young constable to be on guard. When Blathers was nice to him it usually meant he had a plan to trick the lad in some way. "Jerry, will you take some refreshment? Clara, a nice toddy for the constable, and don't spare the rum. If he is required ta sit round here all the day, he should be made as comfortable as possible."

"But, Mr. Blathers, I is on duty, donch ya see."

"Ah, don't ya worry, my boy." Blathers glanced at Alice. "Miss Martin is going to her room to nap. Duff and I," Blathers nodded and grinned at Alice, "are going to our office, as we have work to perform. Clara, I wonder if you and Barkis could spare us a few minutes. Duff and I"—more grinning—"would like to review a few points of our lease with you. Jerry, you just take this lovely beverage, and pull a chair up here. Watch the door. We'll leave the door open so you can see the bottom of the stairs. If there is anyone strange comes in, let out a yell."

We five conspirators adjourned to our office. The properly uniformed constable tilted his chair against the wall, sipped his toddy, and guarded the door.

****

The furniture in our upstairs room is sparse. There is a table we call a desk, and two chairs like the ones in the taproom. Taking into account the number of burns caused by careless smoking, I am sure they spent many years in front of the comfortable fire before being retired for our use. We also have our strongbox. On the one wall, an ancient bookshelf stands precariously. We keep the strongbox on the top shelf. The middle shelf is mine. I have another box, with a cover secured with a leather strap, for the papers I do not need to keep secure in the strongbox. There is also a ledger on my shelf, wherein I keep the financial records of the partnership. Blathers has the lowest shelf. What a mess. He has a box with no lid. Papers are falling out of it because it is so full. He never throws anything away. Next to the box, out in plain sight, he keeps his revolver and the ammunition that goes with it. He also has some books that he slipped into the pocket of his greatcoat when we were working for the Vice Society. We were supposed to destroy the books, but occasionally Blathers would keep one that looked particularly interesting. It didn't make a difference he could not read. They were all written in French. I believe it was the drawings he found most interesting.

The five of us squeezed into the room. The ladies sat in the two chairs. Blathers sat on the top of the desk. Barkis perched on the windowsill. I stood near the door. Blathers said, "Duff, do you want to make a list of the questions we now need to answer?"

“I would very much like to, but, under these conditions, I don’t see how it will be possible.”

“I do,” Barkis said. “There’s a slate and some chalk in the room ’cross the hall. Just one second and I’ll fetch it fer ya.”

That’s when we heard the crash.

Chapter Seventeen

Blathers pushed me aside and ran down the stairs. I was close behind when the step that had caused me to fall earlier came loose again and catapulted me forward. I grabbed onto Blathers' shoulders, but he didn't understand I was losing my balance and shook me loose. Again I hit the wall and fell forward. The board from the stair followed me to the main floor.

By this time, Blathers had gone through the open taproom door. There on the floor, next to an overturned chair, rubbing his eyes, sat a dazed constable.

"What in hell happened here? Was ya attacked, Jerry lad?" Blathers gave up his perfect speech in the heat of the incident.

"No, Mr. Blathers! Me chair slipped out from under me. I don't quite understand it."

"I do." A voice came from a man sitting at a table in the corner, near the open taproom door. "The constable was asleep. I kicked the chair out from under him."

"Oh, gov! Oh, gov. I wasn't asleep, donch ya see. I 'eard the front door open, and I were 'tending ta sleep ta see who were a-comin' in."

"Yes, yes, Constable Cruncher, I know. Now please tell me what was in that glass next to you on the floor; the one you dropped when I kicked the chair. Oh, never mind. I'll speak to you later. Wait outside for me."

The man turned to face me and said, "I'm Inspector Brownlow from Scotland Yard. I want to know what is going on here. From Cruncher's report, it appears that you have kidnapped one Miss Alice Martin. This is a serious offence, and I must ask you two to come along to answer the charge."

By this time, Clara, Barkis and Alice had navigated the damaged stair and entered the room. "I haven't been kidnapped. I came with these gentlemen of my own free will."

"So you are Alice Martin, are you?"

"Yes, I am."

"And, how do I know you are not an imposter, or, if you are the real Alice Martin, how do I know you are now speaking of your own free will? I know kidnappers, and I know their ways. I'm taking these two into custody until I can be sure of the circumstances."

Blathers said, "Now, Inspector, that won't be necessary. My partner and I are acquainted with Sir Robert Peel, you know."

"I don't care if you had breakfast with the Queen. You're coming along now." Brownlow went and opened the front door. Four Bobbies, in addition to Young Jerry Cruncher, came in. "Take these two men to gaol."

Chapter Eighteen

"This cannot happen to an Englishman." Blathers ranted and raved in his Queen's English at the turnkey as he pushed us through the gates of Newgate Prison.

The impingement of his God-given rights offended Blathers. The smell of the place offended me. "We shall have to get out of here soon, or I will never be able to get this odor off me. What causes the place to stink so bad?"

"No one washes, and the food they cook is half of cabbage and half of potatoes."

We were ushered in, in a most uncivil way, by the most ugly and filthy person I have ever seen, to a dingy hole in the wall. "Don't worry, Blathers, I'm sure our friends at the Black Lion will be here shortly with a solicitor and a writ to have us released. We will be back in our office—well, you'll be in the taproom—before teatime."

I may have been a bit optimistic. Teatime came and passed; night fell; the sun rose. Although we did not see the sunrise, I knew it had occurred because I could smell cabbage cooking again. Strangely enough, I guess since we had not had anything to eat for several hours, it started to smell quite good. I hadn't slept, since there was no way I was going to have anything to do with the straw-filled mat that served as a bed. Blathers slept quite well, but now he was scratching in places that polite company might find offensive. He stopped scratching long enough to say, "Let's see if we can find something to eat."

Our cell was part of a larger ward with several other sleeping areas adjoining it. It looked like there was some food and beverage available in the wardroom, so we joined the other prisoners who gathered around a table. "Wot ya in fer?" one hairy fellow without a shirt asked. "Hay ya each killed som'en, or does ya both do the same job?"

I responded, "We haven't killed anyone. We are just here temporarily. There has been a mistake."

"I'll say ya be 'ere just tem'rarely. This be death row. Soon as the warrants come down y'll be swingin' wi' the rest o' us."

Blathers yelled, "Death row? How in the devil did we get on death row? Turnkey, there's been a terrible mistake. Let us out right now. Call the warden. What is going on?"

"Quiet down. There ain't nobody in 'ere what belongs. They're all 'ere cause o' a mistake. I 'spect your papers ta be 'ere today. You'll swing in the morning."

Blathers and I both lost our appetites.

Chapter Nineteen

It was afternoon when the turnkey unlocked the gate to the ward and motioned to us to follow him. To our surprise, he took us to the warden's quarters, where a very sophisticated gentleman greeted us. The turnkey left us, and we were alone with the man. The warden was not in the room.

Blathers asked, "Where is the warden?"

"He has stepped out for the moment, perhaps to respond to a natural need. I am Gabriel Varden. I am in the employ of Sir Robert Peel. Mrs. Clara Barkis has discussed your internment with Lady Peel. I ask you to do exactly as I say. So, if you will, please follow me."

It looked like our expected help was at hand. We followed.

As we proceeded through the prison, all of the gates were open. "Quickly now, follow me." Behold, we were out of gaol.

"There is a coffeehouse just down the street where we can safely talk."

"Coffeehouse! Isn't there a pub nearby? I am half-starved and more thirsty."

"I am sorry, but at the moment security is the most important issue. We know the owners of the coffeehouse and have arranged for a safe place for you to stay for the moment. It is likely your enemies will be after you again soon."

Blathers shrugged, and we went to the establishment Mr. Varden advised. Once seated, he began to explain our situation to us. "You know you were sentenced to hang within the next day or two."

"How can that be? We are entitled to a trial." Blathers still raged about rights as a freeborn Englishman.

"Oh, the record shows there was a trial. A jury of your peers convicted both of you for the murder of Major Martin and the abduction of his sister. Justice Jacob Morgan sentenced you to hang. I'll bet you don't remember the trial, do you?"

"Were we drugged or something? I don't remember anything but being in Newgate."

"You weren't drugged. The papers are fakes. You have some very powerful enemies. We had to get you out of there in a hurry, so the farthest we have planned was to get you safely here. You can't go back to the Black Lion just yet, and you can't go back to your digs. The next attack on you will be less subtle and more deadly."

It was beginning to look like we were doomed to spend the rest of our lives exiled to a coffeehouse, when two patrons we knew quite well came around the corner to the ell where we were sitting. "Thank God, you are free!" Alice hugged Blathers as he rose from his chair. She also put her arm around my shoulder.

Barkis, himself, shook both of our hands. "We came in the cart, soon as we heard ya were here. Mr. Varden had a man watching at the prison gate. Soon as you arrived safely here, he came ta the Lion ta fetch us."

I said, “We are delighted to see you both, and we would love to return to the Black Lion with you, but, alas, it seems we are doomed to remain here for some time.”

Alice said, “We have a plan.”

Chapter Twenty

"First you need a disguise, and I have just the thing. Yesterday, instead of worrying about you two, I went to my brother's flat. With the help of Mr. Barkis, here, I brought all his personal belongings back to the Black Lion. We can use some of his uniforms for a disguise. Mr. Barkis, would you kindly bring in those things we brought in the cart?"

Barkis hurried out to the street and, in a very few minutes, was back with a sack over his shoulder. He and Alice began removing the parts of several military uniforms. "You are going to look lovely in these," she said. "Go in this storage room and try them on."

Blathers and I gathered up the garments and went off to change. When we returned, the inevitable became apparent. The clothes were too short for me and too long for Blathers. "Never mind, I have needle and thread at hand, and we can make sufficient alterations so these uniforms will fit nicely. Because they are uniforms, they are cleverly made to accommodate alterations."

We changed back to our own clothing, and while Alice plied her needle, she explained the second part of her plan. "Now you need a place to sleep for a few days. Is that not so, Mr. Varden?"

"For a few days at least, Miss Martin. We will need

time to deal with the documents that show the convictions. I believe Sir Robert has already sent someone to see Justice Morgan. He will probably assert there was a trial. Then it will be an arduous task to trace down the jurymen that were supposed to have rendered the conviction. We will find some way to expose this travesty, but until then it will be necessary for you gentlemen to be among the missing."

"So here is what I have in mind," Alice said. "I have a very close friend, a draper by trade. His name is George Williams, and he has formed an organization called the Young Men's Christian Association. They have a place where they make rooms available to young men who do not have a residence in London but work here. They are mostly drapers, at this point, and they are very religious. They have Bible readings and the like for their entertainment. It will be a wonderful place to hide you two."

Blathers scratched the back of his neck and looked at the floor. It seemed he wasn't sure which would be worse, the Young Men's Christian Association or the death cell at Newgate. I asked, "Would we be required to attend the Bible sessions or pray any particular prayers? Since our experience with the Vice Society, we are somewhat shy of organized praying."

"Don't worry. I have spoken to Mr. Williams, and Lady Peel has made a sizeable contribution to his organization. He understands your situation. Your rooms will be in the most remote part of their building. Your story is that you are military men suffering from exposure to combat, and you need quiet and rest.

"And now, so you won't be wasting your time, I have prepared some lessons for you to work on, Mr.

Blathers, and for you, Mr. Duff, I have obtained a copy of a recent book by Mr. Thackeray, called *Pendennis.* It should keep you well occupied. Now get into these uniforms, and off you go."

Shortly, two distinguished officers in the service of Her Majesty and the Empire, with caps low on their foreheads and coat collars raised, left the coffeehouse, hailed a cab, and gave an address in The Strand.

Chapter Twenty-One

Life at the Young Men's Christian Association was, shall we say, routine. Yes, routine is the nice thing to say. Most of the residents were country men who came to London seeking employment. The areas where these young impressionable lads could afford lodgings were the sectors where gin shops, bookstores featuring items smuggled from Paris, and prostitutes abounded. Mr. George Williams had founded a place where Christian virtues replaced temptation. He provided daily exercise programs, Bible study, and prayer, accompanied by clean rooms and regular wholesome meals.

I participated in some of the activities. The Bible study sessions were quite informative. The discussions were entirely different from those I recalled from my attendance at the established church as a younger man.

On the other hand, Blathers did nothing but sulk for the first two days. Then he began to pace up and down the hallway outside our room. By the fourth day, he couldn't stand the YMCA, and I couldn't stand him. When he barked, "I needs ta get out o' this here place," I agreed with him. Because of his snoring I had not slept for all the three nights of our stay. I thanked Our Maker that his regular home was at one end of Thames Street and mine was at the other.

“Where are our disguises?” I asked. “I have been thinking it might not be a bad idea to visit Squod. Barkis sends him something against his mortgage each month, so I sent a note to Barkis and obtained information about Squod’s current place of abode. It’s just toward Dover, in a little place called Lindenhurst. We can take the train as soon as we find our disguises. You look for them while I have a word with Mr. Williams. We don’t want him to think us ungrateful for his hospitality, even though you haven’t said a civil word to him since our arrival.”

To this little speech my partner responded in his usual fashion. He grunted. But as soon as we were once again in uniform and on the street headed for the train station, the black cloud around his head began to turn white.

Chapter Twenty-Two

Squod lived near the second to last station on the train line to Dover. When we reached Lindenhurst, we took lodgings for the night at the only inn. Our plan, which I outlined for Blathers during the train trip, was to hire a gig and drive out to confront Squod in the afternoon. We would then stay the night at the inn and take the morning train back to London. Because we were so conspicuous in our red coats, we each brought along our usual clothing to wear while in the town. I felt, and Blathers agreed, that being so far from London we were in no danger from our enemies. That was an error.

"We would like accommodations for the night," I told the landlord at the inn.

"I have two rooms just up the stairs, lookin' out on the street. Or ya can save a bit by sharing the room at the back."

"We will take the two rooms, thank you." I needed a good rest. I was tired of burying my head in pillows.

Once in our rooms, we quickly changed out of our uniforms and met in the taproom of the inn. Apparently it takes me a bit more time to attire myself, as Blathers was just finishing a pint when I arrived. "Are you ready?" I asked.

Blathers wiped his mouth with the back of his

hand. “Ready as I’ll ever be.”

We were off. We rented a fine gig from the inn’s hostler. Unfortunately, the horse was somewhat of a disappointment. “We should ha’ brought old Pincher. Even at his age he would be better than this here nag.”

“I agree, but of course neither of us would ask good old Pincher to make such a journey.”

“Right ya are. Yoho, there, ya bag o’ bones.”

The trip took longer than we anticipated because of the horse, but we finally found the cottage where Squod had retired. Once again our plan failed. Squod had not changed, except now he was well inebriated in the late afternoon instead of waiting until the evening. We tried asking him a few questions.

“Squod, do you remember us, Blathers and Duff?”

“Ah, the rozzers. I doesn’t know nothin’ ’bout Jack. I hasn’t seen him since ya two ran him inta hidin’.” He drank from the bottle in front of him on the table.

“We doesn’t want ta talk about Jack this time. We wants ta know ’bout diamonds.” Blathers had reverted to his former way of speaking. Alice wasn’t present, and there was no need for airs in front of Squod.

Squod took another long pull on the bottle. His head bobbed toward the table. Then he sat bolt upright. “Diamonds? Oh, diamonds. Is ya workin’ fer the Order now?”

“What Order?”

“Ya must know ’bout the Order if ya knows ’bout the diamonds.”

“We want you to tell us all you know, to verify what we know is true.”

Squod drank again, and this time his head hit the

table. Once again he sat up. “I can’t remember now. Come back in the mornin’ and I’ll tells ya all ’bout it.” His head hit the table for the last time.

Chapter Twenty-Three

Because the front rooms of the inn looked east, the bright sunlight woke me early. It was not a problem. I had just enjoyed my first good sleep in several days. As I prepared to dress, I heard the train taking passengers to Dover for the morning packet to France. It made a stop at the station across from the hotel. Two men dressed in heavy coats, with the collars turned up, got down from the train. In a matter of minutes a coach pulled up, and they both climbed aboard. The coach drove out of town in the same direction Blathers and I had gone on the previous day.

I joined Blathers in the taproom, and we breakfasted on kippers and scrambled eggs. Blathers finished his meal before I did. He said, "I'm goin' ta step out and see that hostler about gettin' a better horse fer today."

"Very good idea. I will be along shortly. I require more tea, and I doubt Squod will be up too early. We should still be able to catch him before he passes out."

****

The new horse was a great improvement. Blathers said, "I picked her out meself. That hostler tried to stick me wi' another nag, but I wouldn't have it." Blathers did know about horses. We proceeded along without incident until we saw a coach coming toward us at a dangerous pace. Fortunately, Blathers' driving skills saved us from what could have been a serious accident.

"Them fellas was sure in a rush."

"I think it was the coach I saw leaving the village before breakfast this morning. It was carrying two men who just arrived on the Dover train."

"Wonder whats they was up to."

"Blathers, you should still try to speak as Miss Martin has taught you, even though she is not present. You will never get in the habit of speaking properly unless you try all of the time."

"I knows, I mean, I know. I'll try."

I believe Blathers was doing his best, but it was clear he would let down unless he could actually see Miss Martin. Perhaps he felt no one else cared. I wanted to show him I cared.

He got the gig back on the road, and within a few minutes Squod's cottage was in view. He was apparently expecting us because the door was open. While Blathers saw to the horse, I knocked on the open door. "Mr. Squod, it's Blathers and Duff back, as you suggested yesterday." As I stuck my head into the room I was hoping he remembered yesterday. That's when I discovered he not only would not remember yesterday, but he would not have a tomorrow.

Blathers was now right behind me. "Holy, will ya look at that, now!"

Squod's head, or what was left of it, was in the fireplace. There must have been some embers still smoldering from last night's fire, for I could smell burning hair. His arms were bent in all different directions. I thought they were no longer attached to the body. It must have been a brutal beating. Squod was clutching a paper in his right hand. Blathers opened the fist and took out the paper. He started to hand it to me when he remembered he could read.

"There's one of them, those Maltese crosses on the paper, just like on the coded message. All it says is 'Traitor.' Look at that, all the fingers on his left hand are broken backward. The poor slob didn't die easy."

I told Blathers, "I think those men in the coach did this. They must have found out Squod was going to talk to us. We should get out of here and not return to the village. They might be looking for us there."

"Ah, let's look around here for a bit before we take off, then, There must be something about we can use to our advantage. Do you want to stand guard while I look, or do you want to look while I guard?"

"Let's take turns."

"Good idea." Blathers went looking through the cottage while I stood by the door watching for anyone approaching. It would not do for us to be accused of another murder. When he finally came to the door, he carried a small sack. "What do you have there?"

"Diamonds! I'll show you when we get away from here. Now hurry. Take a look around and remember everything you see." Blathers calls my excellent memory for details my "mind's eye."

Chapter Twenty-Four

It was fortunate we had given up our rooms at the inn and brought our cases with us, for we decided we would continue on to Dover and take the train back to London from there. If the killers were seeking us, they would be waiting for us in Lindenhurst. If we took the train from Dover, it might not even stop at Lindenhurst.

The trip to Dover was quite a bit farther than back to the village, but Blathers assured me the horse was capable of the journey. At Dover we paid for the livery stable to return the horse and gig to Lindenhurst and purchased tickets to London.

"We would like to go on the express train, please."

"There's no more express till the mornin'. Ya kin take the local at half-two or ya kin stay the night at the hotel and take the half-seven express in the mornin'."

"We'll take the local. Two tickets, please."

The wait until the train left was short, and the ride to Lindenhurst, the next stop, was less than thirty minutes. It was when we stopped at Lindenhurst that I wished we had stayed over and taken the morning train. At Lindenhurst, two passengers boarded.

"Are those the gents you saw?"

"That's them. Do you think we should get off?"

"No, they may be looking for us, but they might not know what we look like. They might be looking for two mates in soldier suits. Let's sit tight and try to see if we can learn anything."

The train chugged on. It was only two more stations when a man dressed in tweeds, like he was coming off a day of shooting, boarded the train and struck up a conversation with the suspected killers. He looked like I should know him, but of course I didn't. My contacts with country people were very few. He got off after three stops, still deep in the country. After that though, the two brutes seemed to take more of an interest in Blathers and me. "Blathers, I think we should make a hasty exit from this train at the very next stop and see what happens. I don't like the way those two are looking at us now."

Chapter Twenty-Five

As the train approached the next stop, I rose and went to the rear of the car. Blathers went to the front. The stop was very brief. There was only one passenger waiting to board. The train began to start forward. One of the thugs was watching me, and one was watching Blathers. Momentum began to build, and Blathers yelled, "Look out!" and pointed to the rear of the car. At the same time I yelled, "Look out!" and pointed to the front of the car. Heads began to spin. The train gained speed, and my partner and I stood on the station platform, waving. "Ta-ta!"

Now, of course, we had increased peril to face. Persons who we believed were killers were chasing us. The authorities wanted us for escaping from jail, at the very least, and we had no idea where we were. Blathers, always the practical one said, "Let's wait for the next train." So wait we did.

The next local left Dover at half-five. The long time between trains offered an opportunity to review our situation and, at least mentally, make a list of the facts of the case as we knew them. There was, however, one thing bothering me. I asked, "Blathers, that fellow on the train talking to those two ruffians—did he look familiar to you?"

"Can't say as he did, but he must have knowed us,

'cause there's no doubt he pointed us out to them hooligans."

This was not a good time to speak to Blathers about his grammatical errors, and there was one other thing we needed to discuss. "No doubt. Now, while we're waiting, tell me about the diamonds you found."

"It was a small bag tucked in a straw mattress on a cot in the loft. There are about five stones in it, and they all seem to be diamonds."

"I wonder where Squod got those."

"Probably stole them from the stash supposed to be at the inn."

"It seems his killers must not have known there were any diamonds there."

"Or else they had to leave in a hurry."

"Well, let's recapitulate what we know while we wait."

"Sure, I never recapitulated afore. Do you have something to write on, so we has, have a list?"

"No!" I didn't want to get into the old argument about the effectiveness of my methods. "We can just discuss what we know, and I'll make a list later."

"I'd prefer to discuss what we don't know, if you please. Like who or what is this Order that seems to be causing all the trouble, with their little cross."

"The clue is the little cross. I understand there are some semi-religious, semi-military groups that think they are descended from the Crusaders, and who use a cross like that as a symbol. I think it appears in the sign of the Black Lion because that was one of their meeting places. Squod was certainly a member, but that sign is older than he is."

"Maybe the membership is passed down from

father to son, and the Black Lion Inn was passed with it."

"That could be the case. When Squod's son was thought to be a killer…"

"Killer? You mean a bloody maniac."

"Yes, maniac. In any event, when he disappeared, he probably forfeited his right, and perhaps Squod got in bad with the Order."

"The Order, the Order. Who the devil is the Order? Do you think those ruffians are part of the Order?"

"I think they may be, or they may be hired thugs, but the fellow that met them on the train probably was part of the Order. I still think he was someone we know, but the clothing didn't seem right. That full beard, it could have been a fake."

"If ya see him again, let me know. I'll walk up and yank on his whiskers."

Chapter Twenty-Six

When we reached London we weren't much closer to solving the perplexing questions that faced us. We also had another quandary to resolve. "Where do you think we should go now?" I asked Blathers.

"Not back to the YMCA. It was nice of them to put us up, but except for the hanging part, I preferred Newgate."

We decided to try to sneak into the Black Lion. We took an omnibus to a stop two blocks from the Inn and traveled by back alleys until we reached the back door that entered on Barkis' private rooms. This was the same door Jack Squod had used to make his escape, and Lady Peel had used when meeting with us at the inn. It took some time before anyone heard our knocking, but at last Barkis, himself, answered.

Blathers said, "Barkis, don't say a word. Just nod. Is that Inspector Brownlow or any of his Bobbies around?"

"Omygosh! I was just having a little nap when I dreamt I heard a knocking."

"No, no. Quiet now."

"Oh, it's all right. There's no one here 'cept that Mr. Varden, and he has some good news. He has got ya cleared of all the crimes ya committed. Come in, now. Everyone is in the taproom."

And there they were, including the very dapper Gabriel Varden. He rose from the table and shook each of our hands. Alice gave Blathers a big hug and a kiss on the cheek. Blathers turned red. Alice took my hand and gave it a tender squeeze. Clara remained in her chair. Once she was tucked in, she couldn't untuck without making a great effort. But she wiggled and reached out to us with both hands. I bent to her so she could hug me. Blathers only waved. He headed toward the taps with Barkis, himself.

Gabriel Varden said, "We have been worried about you two. We went to Mr. Williams' establishment to tell you Sir Robert has been able to convince Justice Morgan that there was an error in his records. The justice apologizes. You were apparently confused with two other criminals named Boomers and Ruff. Believe that if you will. Of course, Sir Robert is quite certain the honorable justice is involved in this mischief somehow, but for political reasons he is not able to publicize the man's treachery."

Alice asked, "Where have you two been?"

We took turns telling about our adventure to see Squod, and our encounter with the team of killers.

Then Barkis dropped a heavy cloth purse on the table. "I was repairing the stairway and found this under the stairway." He produced his hammer as evidence of his labors. "They were under that stair that's been causing everyone to fall."

Blathers went to the chair where he had left his coat and pulled an identical but less heavy sack from its pocket.

Chapter Twenty-Seven

Gabriel held up the two bags, side by side. Blathers told everyone where he had found his treasure and that it contained some diamonds. Barkis laughed. "This here bag is full of diamonds. Isn't it, Mr. Varden?"

Varden grimaced. "We sure thought so." He opened the bag and placed one of the diamonds on the table in front of the detectives. He picked up Barkis' hammer and crashed it down on the jewel. It disintegrated into powder. "Paste! I took these to the jeweler that Sir Robert relies on. He assured me they are all paste. Now let's test Mr. Blathers' find." He took a stone from Blathers sack, placed it on the table, and smashed it. The diamond remained undamaged. "Ah, the real thing." Varden took a knife from the pocket of his frock coat and pried the gem out of the tabletop. "Sorry to have damaged your furniture, Mrs. Barkis."

"Don't think a thing about it, Mr. Varden. That table has been dented a thousand times by all sorts of mugs."

Varden asked me what I thought of the situation. Well, he really asked both Blathers and me, but I surmised that Blathers might need more time to develop an idea, so I jumped in with my thoughts. "If I wanted to guess, I would say Squod took the diamonds the Order left with him and spent them, at least most of them. He fooled the other members by substituting paste. Thus, a full bag of paste, with a small number of actual diamonds remaining."

Blather agreed with me. "Yes, and it is a good bet the damn Order, whoever they are, was good and fooled, because they are looking here, but they didn't search Squod's place."

Alice was downhearted. "All this means is that my brother was murdered for a sack of paste and a few measly stones. I wish neither he nor I had ever seen that silly cryptic note."

Blathers put his arms around her and held her close. That's when young Edward Childers strode into the taproom. "Take your hands of that girl, you old lecher." He grabbed Blathers' arm and spun him away from Alice. And her tears really began to flow.

Chapter Twenty-Eight

Clara struggled out of her chair and buried the lachrymose lady in her bosom. Blathers was preparing to place young Childers' teeth in the back of his throat, but Mr. Varden stepped between the two. "Now, now, gentlemen, none of that. You, young man, what is the meaning of this intrusion?"

"Alice, Miss Martin and I are…" He paused. "I am…" Another pause. "We are…" He shrugged. "We're very close friends. I don't like seeing her pawed by the likes of him. I see how he looks at her. I don' want him touching her. If he does, I'll…"

Blathers raised his fist again. "You'll do what? You young dandies think you're something, but all you have to do is take off your dandy coat, and I'll give you a dandy sleep. What do you think a fine woman like Miss Martin would see in a sissy toff like you?"

Varden said, "Please, now, that will be enough from both of you. What is your name, young man?"

"Edward Childers. My father is Harold Childers, the industrialist. You may have heard of him."

"That Childers. Yes, indeed, I have heard of him. Now, Mr. Blathers was simply attempting to comfort the young lady. I am quite sure his motives were honorable. So what exactly is your claim to her, that can justify your behavior?"

"Miss Martin was in the employ of my family, and my father and I have taken on the responsibility for her wellbeing."

At that moment, Harold Childers burst into the room. "What are you doing here again, Edward?"

"Father, are you following me?"

"Never mind. Answer me. Have I not forbidden you to come here?"

"But I love Alice. I have come here to ask her to marry me. Alice, will you marry me?"

Alice stopped sobbing, took a deep breath, looked at the floor, sighed, and looked at young Childers. "Edward, I am very fond of you. I may even love you, but I can never marry you. I would never be happy living the life you would expect of me if I were your wife. I want to live so that at the end of my day I can say I have helped someone live better. I cannot do this if I marry you."

This little speech deeply affected two people. Edward Childers became downcast, as could be expected. What I did not expect was to see Blathers' reaction. His eyes watered, and he stared at the young lady. After all these years, Blathers was in love.

But Alice was not finished with her announcement. "I should also tell you all, since you have all been so kind to me and become my closest friends, I do intend to marry. Before this all started, I promised to wed with George Williams, the man Mr. Blathers and Mr. Duff know from the YMCA."

Blathers' expression changed from melancholy to astonishment. Alice noticed the change. "Oh, don't worry, Mr. Blathers. I will continue to tutor you until you can read and write as well as Mr. Dickens himself."

Chapter Twenty-Nine

Childers, the elder, noticed the two bags on the table. "I say, what have we here?" He went to grab at the bags, but Gabriel Varden scooped them up first. "Just some things that belong to me," he said. He put both bags in an inside pocket of his coat.

"By Jove, those look like sacks that would contain a king's ransom, from the time of Richard the Lion-hearted, don't you know." Harold Childers had once again adopted his public school style of speaking, which was set aside while he was chastising his son. "I say, I am most interested in historical things, you know. May I have a look at your sacks?"

Varden replied, "Some other time. At this moment, they contain some personal items I would prefer not to display."

"Oh, well then, by Jove, we shall be shoving off, as they say in the Navy. Come along, Edward."

Edward was so despondent he simply followed his father to the door without a word. Once they were gone, Clara again hugged Alice, and Barkis, himself, patted her back. Clara said, "We're so happy you will be wed to a nice man. We know you still grieve for the loss of your brother, but having a lovely husband will help heal all wounds." She glanced at Barkis, himself.

Blathers said, "This is all well and good, but we

still have a mystery and two murders to solve. Let's get down to business."

It's unlikely Blathers will ever fall in love again.

It had been an emotional meeting for Alice, so Clara took her to her room to rest. Barkis had a carting job. He went off to hitch up his team. That left Blathers, Gabriel Varden, and me. Varden suggested, "Let's retire to your room upstairs. We can discuss the situation without interruption and find a safe place to hide these." He produced the two bags from the inside of his coat.

Chapter Thirty

When we were settled in our room, I took out a pad of paper, a pen, and some ink.

"Oh, jeez, here he goes making his lists again," my grumpy partner said.

"It is not my fault you don't have a wife, so do not be upset with me."

"A wife! What kind of a life would it be if'n I were stuck wi' a wife?"

"And do not go back to talking as though you did not know better."

Varden said, "Gentlemen, shall we focus on the problems at hand?"

Blathers said. "Right, let's get on with it. How much would those fake diamonds be worth if they were not paste?"

Varden answered, "I asked my jeweler friend. He wasn't sure because there is a difference in value based on any number of factors, like clarity, size of the individual stones, and so on. He did say, however, that they would be worth at least half a million pounds."

Blathers scratched the back of his neck. "Well, now, that's just the thing. Do you think old Squod drank up a half a million pounds of diamonds?"

I just struck me how ridiculous that would be. "If he did, he surely would have died a long time before he was murdered."

"Then what happened to them? Or, more correct, the money they were sold for?"

"Who else would have known about them?"

Varden asked, "Who else lived with Squod?"

We both said together, "Jack Squod."

I explained to Varden about our first visit to the old inn, and how Jack had disappeared into the depths of London. "It has been over ten years now, and there has been no word of him, although there has been the occasional killing similar to the murder here." I pointed through the open door to the room across the hallway.

Varden shook his head. "We could begin a search for him, but with half a million pounds he could be living anywhere in the world."

Blathers said, "He could also hide out very well right here in London. If some of those killings that looked like his *were* his, it might be that is just what he's doing. I wonder who will be at old Squod's burial?"

Chapter Thirty-One

I don't think anyone was surprised that the morning was dark and drizzly when Squod was laid to rest. It is always like that. There was a preacher because the old sot had maintained his rates with the parish. There was an undertaker and hired men to carry the casket. Someone was paying them. There was Varden under one black umbrella. There I was under another. There was Blathers huddled with his coat collar raised around his neck. He wouldn't use an umbrella. He was afraid one of the spokes would poke his eye out. The only other mourners were two women, each standing alone under separate black umbrellas. One was quite elderly, the other younger looking but attired in such a way that it was difficult to guess an age. There was no sign of Jack Squod.

The elderly lady stood not far away from and slightly ahead of Blathers. The prayers were over in short order. The hired men lowered the casket, and the undertaker threw a symbolic shovel of dirt on it. The service was so short Blathers was hardly damp. As the elderly woman turned toward her carriage, she was facing Blathers. He said, "It was nice of you to come. I don' believe I have had the pleasure of your acquaintance," just like he was family of the deceased.

The lady bowed her head slightly. "I am Phil's

wife, what left him so many years ago and run off with a traveling man. You aren't me own son Jack, is ya?"

"No, madam. I was an acquaintance of Mr. Squod when he owned the Black Lion."

"Oh, dear! I comes here taday in hopes me own son, what I hasn't seen all these years, would be at his own father's burial. I has hoped ta see him one more time afore I passes meself."

Just then, the other woman hurried toward Blathers and the old lady. As she neared them, she lowered her umbrella and folded it. Then she raised the folded umbrella, like she intended to strike the old lady, but then lowered it and strode away.

She crossed the grass, jumped on a horse tethered near the cemetery gate, and rode off like an accomplished horseman.

"Horse*man*!" Blathers said. "There goes Jack Squod."

Chapter Thirty-Two

We helped the old lady to her carriage and invited her to take lunch with us at the inn where the three of us had taken rooms for the evening. Blathers rode with her. Varden and I followed in the coach that had brought us to the graveyard.

We were all chilled from our experience in the misty rain. I was happy to have a cup of hot strong tea. Mrs. Squod, for we discovered she had never remarried, joined me. Of course Blathers had a large brandy and Varden did the same. Settled near the fire in the lounge with our warming beverages, we prevailed upon Mrs. Squod to tell her story. As it turned out, she would have done so had we never asked.

"I were a young girl when we was wed and Jack were born. Phil were a fine man, 'cept when he were drinkin'. Then long come this here quite han'some, smooth-talkin' feller. And I falls fer him."

She ran off with the chap, who was a seller of medicines. It was a few years before she realized he had women in several places. When he needed or wanted to visit the other women, he would stick her in a cheap hotel for a few weeks. Quite often, upon his return, they would be obligated to leave the hotel in the middle of the night because of a lack of funds. Finally, he failed to return for her. She had no money and nowhere to go.

But the landlord of the hotel had a plan for her. She stayed as a tenant until she was no longer attractive. She then moved to a closet in the kitchen where she washed floors and dishes for the patrons, including the young woman who took her room.

"At first, I tries ta go back ta Phil, but he would have none of it. He gets drunk and he beats me while young Jack sits there a-lookin'. It were horrible."

She returned to the hotel of ill repute and had been there all the time since, doing the dirty work. "I doesn't thinks I can last much longer. When I hears that Phil is dead, I thinks this will be me last chance ta ever see young Jack again. The landlord—he's not such a bad feller—lent me the money ta come here. You say that woman at the grave were me own Jack? Were he gonna hit me? Why would he does such a thing?"

I said, "I believe it was Jack, yes. He seemed angry."

"I doesn't blame him. Poor boy!"

I wanted to find out if Mrs. Squod knew anything about the Maltese cross on the sign of the Black Lion or about the Order.

"Mrs. Squod, on the sign at the Black Lion, the lion is holding a cross. Do you have any idea of its significance?"

"Nifigance. What does ya mean, nifigance?"

"I'm sorry. I mean, do you know why there is a cross on the sign?"

"Oh, the cross. It had ta do wi' the Order, ya know."

"I see. What Order?"

"Oh, them malty mates of Phil's. They was always shuttin' down the taproom fer their meetin's. There were some tough fellers in that bunch, but there were a few swells, as well. I al'as thinks they was up ta no good."

"By 'malty' do you mean Maltese?"

"Yes. Well, I doesn't say it so good. I hasn't had mush schoolin', ya knows."

"Do you know the name of any of the members of the Order?"

"They all had nicknames, ya know. I know Phil were called Landlord."

"Do you remember any of the other nicknames?"

"Oh, let me see. There were two big fellas. They calls them the Twins. Then there were Banker. He were a dandy and kinda were leader o' the bunch. I doesn't remembers any more. They all had names like people's work, ya know."

Chapter Thirty-Three

We had acquired quite a bit of information to date, but it was, at this point, a hodgepodge. Regardless of the fuss Blathers made over my habit of arranging information in lists, I knew I had to do it. Therefore, I was in our room at the Black Lion early on the day following our return from Squod's interment. I knew Blathers would not arrive before half-ten. He had arranged for a lesson with Miss Martin. I had all morning to put some order to the clues we had acquired.

Those who try to lead orderly lives, like myself, will know the first step in any task is to be sure that the needed tools or supplies are at hand. I arranged pens, fresh ink, and paper on the tabletop. I felt the first category on my list should be about the Order, since yesterday's discussion with Mrs. Squod was fresh in my mind. I began:

The Order

1. The Order used a Maltese cross as a symbol of identification.
2. Squod was a member of the Order, known as the Landlord.
3. It is likely a Maltese cross appears in the sign of the Black Lion because of Squod's membership.

I was thinking about how to arrange the

information obtained from Mrs. Squod when there was a knock on my door. “I say, old chap, lovely morning, what? The landlady said I could find you here. A bit of a word, if you have the time.” Childers Senior poked his head into the room.

“Why, yes, please come in and have a seat.”

“Very decent, of you, old chap. May I close the door?” Before I could answer, the door slammed shut. “I wish to speak to you about the two little sacks that were on the table in the taproom yesterday.” I was looking at a quite large pistol in the good old fellow’s hand. “I would certainly dislike having to use this weapon, so I will appreciate your cooperation. Do you understand, old chap?” The tone of the term “old chap” had changed to threatening.

“I know nothing about those bags. They were the property of the other gentleman, Mr. Varden.”

“Have you seen Mr. Varden today?”

“No.”

“And you won’t. He is in hospital. Apparently two brigands attacked him as he was leaving here yesterday.”

“The Twins.”

“So you have heard of the Twins?”

My revelation seemed to surprise Childers. I thought I would try to rattle him a little further. “Yes, I know about the Twins, and I know about the Banker, as well.” As I said this, it hit me: Harold Childers was the man on the train, the one I thought I recognized. He had worn a disguise, but there are certain features that often show through any disguise. I now saw those features in the man holding a gun on me. The threatening look in the eyes was one of those features. If I continued to disclose what I thought I knew, I increased the chances the look would turn into action, and I would be fortunate if I turned up in hospital next to Varden. The undertaker was the other possibility.

I decided to take my chances. Maybe if I pushed the villain he would run instead of pulling the trigger. "I also know you were with the Twins on the train right after they murdered Squod. They were acting on your instruction. It is also likely you killed Major Martin. How many others have you killed? You must have disposed of quite a few other members of the Order to gain sole possession of the diamonds." It seemed from the moment Childers pulled his gun, my mind started listing all the facts, which led to the conclusions now spilling, almost uncontrollably, from my lips. "The diamonds were the treasury of the Order, weren't they?" I started to guess. "One of the Order's businesses was smuggling diamonds. What else did you smuggle? Women from China for the brothels of Limehouse? Did you carry slaves to the West Indies? How about liquor from Europe?"

The more that came out of my mouth, the closer the gun came to a point between my eyes.

Chapter Thirty-Four

I had just about decided I had guessed too well when the door opened. "This here young—what the…" Blathers and young Edward Childers pushed into the room.

"Father, what are you doing?"

The gun-wielding Childers turned at the intrusion, just enough for me to give him a shove toward the wall. It wasn't enough. He turned and smacked my head with the weapon. Blathers lunged for him but missed. He pushed Blathers into me and jumped toward the door. At the head of the stairway, he turned and fired. Young Edward reeled and fell to the floor.

The father either didn't realize he had hit his son or he didn't care. He started to run down the stairs. The third board from the top came loose, and Harold Childers, still clutching his gun with two hands, fell forward, landing at the base of the stairway looking like bones in a bag of skin.

Chapter Thirty-Five

Of course, you wish to know who lived and who died. Young Edward suffered a wound to his shoulder. Blathers and I were able to stop the bleeding and get him to hospital. He ended up in the same ward as Gabriel Varden. Harold Childers broke his neck in the fall. When we got around to him, Barkis was standing over him, hammer in hand, waiting for him to be moved so he could repair the stair. Childers was already dead when we reached him. We called the Metropolitan Police to clean up.

A few days later, I went from the office to the taproom at about half eleven. Soon after I got there, Gabriel Varden came in. He wore a bandage on his head. He was using crutches, as his leg was in splints. The area around his left eye was still discolored. Of course, Blathers sat with both hands wrapped around a pewter mug. Clara, Barkis, himself, and Alice Martin, along with Mr. Dickens and his good friend John Forester, were also in attendance. Varden had a brandy, and I accepted tea.

All eyes were on Varden as he reported on the events that had occurred since the death of Harold Childers. "The Twins were nabbed by the Bobbies and are going to swing from two ropes together. The Order, which was nothing more than a gang of criminals, has been put out of business. The police have matched up some of their unsolved murders with persons who may have been members of the Order."

I was quite pleased at this information. It confirmed that the guesses I had hurled at Childers were correct.

Varden went on. "Young Childers is still in hospital. It appears he will be there for some time. I spoke with him before I left. Neither he nor his mother knew anything about his father's activities. They thought him simply a very successful businessman. He says when he is recovered he will devote his life to the care of his mother. He seems to be leaning toward preparing for the priesthood. Well, we'll see. That would be quite a change in lifestyle for him.

"There is one remaining matter. The few real diamonds are worth about ten thousand pounds. What shall become of them? Does anyone feel they have a right to the stones?"

No one spoke.

"In that case, I suggest they be sold and the proceeds be given to Mr. George Williams for his work in the Young Men's Christian Association. It seems to me the idea behind the organization is a sound one, and the concept may spread to other areas. Why, someday there may be a YMCA in several cities in England."

TALE FOUR

Four Visits to a Whorehouse
Spring 1855

Get thee to a brothel.

Chapter One
The First Visit

When I got to the taproom, everyone was adither. Duff yelled at me, "Blathers, where have you been?"

"What do you mean, where have I been? I never get here early unless we are working on a case. You know that." Clara Barkis, landlady of the Black Lion Inn, was in tears. Another lady, who I didn't know but she looked somewhat like Clara, was weeping away as well. I say somewhat like Clara because Clara is a bit on the heavy side, between 18 and 20 stone. This other lady had Clara's features but was a wispy little woman.

I asked, "Duff, what have you done to Clara and this here lady?" Clara continued to sob. Duff shrugged. The little lady wailed. Clara wanted to tell me all about the problem but kept sobbing instead.

I'll try to tell you what it was without all the crying, and wringing of hands, and wiping of the eyes. It'll go much quicker. The gist of it is, the little woman was Clara's sister, Miss Betsey Peggotty. Eighteen years ago, she took in this orphan girl and raised her up. The girl was thought to be the baby daughter of Lizabeth Stride. The tart they called Little Liz on the street, who was bloody murdered upstairs in this very inn.

Now the young girl, a full-grown lady, left

Betsey's home in Dover to make her own way in London. All the crying was because she had disappeared.

I didn't know what was wrong with Duff. We've been partners since we were in the Bow Street Runners, and I hadn't seen him like this in a long time. He's usually the one does the organizing of facts of our cases. He makes his lists and all, to help us see what is there to see. Now he was just pacing around rubbing his eyes. It's almost like the time young Joe, the pickpocket, got beat up by some thugs and died in Duff's arms. I said, "Duff, settle down, lad. If we are to help, we need to get some information here. Have you made a list of what it is we know, and what it is we don't know?" Duff just shook his head. He was going to be no use. The lot of them wouldn't be of much use the way they were. I didn't know what to do to settle them down, until Mr. Dickens came in for his noon meal.

Now, I must tell you, it is because of Mr. Dickens I am writing this all down. He has led me to believe he can make me a well-known author, if I write about the adventures of Blathers and Duff. You should also know it is because of Alice Martin I am able to write so correct. She is the one who taught me the proper way to speak and write.

Dickens asked me what was all the trouble. I told him, "There's a young girl as has gone missing. I been trying to get some details, so I would know how to go about finding her, but all I'm getting is sobs and sobs."

"Well, then, will I be able to get a meal, Mrs. Barkis?"

That took care of things. As soon as everyone

noticed the arrival of Mr. Dickens, they straightened right out.

Clara said, "Oh, certainly, Mr. Dickens, please excuse us, and sit yourself down. Will you be wanting a drink of something? Jane has just come in. She's a wee late again today. But I'll have her right out with your meal."

"A pint of bitter, please, Mrs. Barkis, and some of your lovely shepherd's pie if you have it." Jane brought in the pint and a plate of steaming pie. She smiled at Dickens, and the famous writer put his hand on her arm as she set the plate down.

"Now, Blathers, Duff, tell me about your predicament."

I said, "Right. Duff, stop your wailing, and tell us what you know, now."

Duff took a deep breath. "I was only here a short time when Clara's sister arrived from Dover. She took the morning train. It seems that about a month ago she and the girl, I think her name is Emma, had a disagreement and decided it was time for her to move. She and Miss Peggotty mended their differences, but, nonetheless, they agreed that Emma would come to London to make her way. Miss Peggotty says she is a beautiful and well-educated girl. She was not surprised to have a letter from Emma telling her that she had secured a position as a governess to two small children. The girl wrote to Miss Peggotty twice a week, and Miss Peggotty wrote back. Then, earlier this week, when the young lady was to take up her position, no letters arrived. Miss Peggotty's last post came back with the notation, 'not known at this address.' She wrote to Colonel Granger, the girl's employer, but that letter came back with the same notation."

Dickens asked, "What was the address of this Colonel Granger?" He took out his notebook and made a note of the name. "Always looking for colorful names."

Duff turned to Clara's sister. "Miss Peggotty, do you have the address you used for corresponding with your ward?"

"I do. It is right here in my reticule." She extracted an envelope from her purse and handed it to Duff. Duff handed it to Dickens, and Dickens handed it to me. I took a notebook from my pocket and noted the address:

Miss Emma Peggotty
Bliss House
5 Northwick Terrace
St. John's Wood
Westminster

****

The house was a three-story town house. It was very fashionable, with Greek pillars on the front and windows rounded at the top. I knocked on the front door with the big brass knocker set just below a small window. No answer. I knocked harder, maybe a little too hard for such a fancy establishment. Finally, a part of a face appeared in the little window, and the door opened.

He was a giant, at least seven feet tall, and there wasn't a hair on his head, not even eyebrows. He was wearing a lemon yellow silk shirt and cherry red trousers. The shirt was tight, and I could see his muscles ripple under it.

I took a step backwards, and he said, "Come back at six. They're all still asleep."

I said, "I want…"

He said, "I know what you want. Come back at six," and closed the door.

I would have knocked again, but I didn't want to make a pest of myself. Since the place looked high-class, I needed to act high-class so I wouldn't be sent around back to the tradesmen's entrance. I remember Duff saying that discretion is the art of princes and kings and decided I would be discreet and come back at six.

A few blocks away I found a less distinguished neighborhood and a tavern where I could be comfortable. I passed the time until six with beer and darts. Just before leaving I had a bit of cheese and cold ham, just to reestablish my discretioness.

****

Back at Bliss House, the Metropolitan Police were all over the street and in the house. My favorite young Peeler—well, not so young any more—Jerry Cruncher was guarding the entrance to the house. The conversation went something like this.

"Well, Young Jerry, still guarding the scene of the crime, are you?"

"I been doin' this fer eighteen years now, Mr. Blathers. It seems ta suit me, donch ya see."

"Much like your dad standing outside Tellson's bank all those years. How is your dad then, Young Jerry?"

"Ah, 'e passed this time last year. And, wouldn't ya know it, someone stole his body out o' the grave. It was a sad thin' all together. Mum couldn't understand 'ow a thin' like that could 'appen. She flopped down and prayed 'is body would come back."

"I myself am sad to here that, Young Jerry, or should we now stop calling you Young Jerry?"

"Since the old Jerry is gone, just plain Jerry will do. Or you might think o' callin' me constable when I is in uniform."

"What has happened here then, Young Jerry?"

Jerry took a deep breath and shook his head. "There 'as been a murder, Mr. Blathers, and that's all I can tell ya. Me orders are to keep folks away, and under no circumstances to let a'body inta the 'ouse. Now please move along, and no tricks."

"But Jerry, I have business in the house."

"Well, I never suspected ya was that kind a person, but I guesses ya 'as to go somewhere when ya gets the urge. Only I wouldn't think ya could 'fford a place like this."

I didn't know what the lad was talking about, but I needed to get into that house. I had tricked Young Jerry so many times he was on his guard. I thought of a few possibilities but gave them up. Probably Young Jerry wouldn't believe anything I said, but I was desperate to see what kind of a house it was, and what was going on. If Betsey's ward was in there, she might need some help. Then I remembered the tradesmen's entrance.

****

Sure enough, decked out in his shiny buttons, there was another of Sir Robert's finest standing guard. As soon as I came around the corner I began to half-run toward the guard.

"Constable, Jerry Cruncher needs your help out front. Hurry!" I entered the fine establishment through the tradesmen's entrance.

Once inside, I recognized members of the

Metropolitan Police who I knew and who knew me. It seemed I had two choices. I could either hide out from the coppers or I could pretend I belonged there. I thought the second choice would be more successful. I waved and nodded as seemed necessary and went up to the officer in charge.

"Blathers, what are you doing here?"

"Ah, Inspector Nickleby, I'm doing the same as you, investigating."

"Oh! I remember now. A private investigator, Well, stay out of the way of my men."

While I was talking to the Inspector I could see Young Jerry and the other Bobbie peeking into the front door to see if they were in trouble. I was sure they wouldn't say anything unless their governor noticed something was wrong.

Most of the activity seemed to be on the upper floor. I marched up the center stairway like I belonged. That floor was divided into several rooms, more than you would think it should be, almost like a hotel. All the Metropolitan Police crowded around the entrance to one room. I thought it would be likely someone would ask why I was there if I tried to push my way in, so I decided to explore the next floor up. That's how I finally realized what kind of a house it was.

This floor was also fitted out like a hotel. All the doors were closed except one, and there she sat on the end of the bed. She was wearing a thin robe, and I could see right through it. She smiled at me. "Are you looking for me?" She dropped the top of her robe to her waist.

I stood firm. Against the temptation, I mean. "Are you Emma?"

"No. I'm Kit. Emma is the third door on the floor

below. But I wouldn't go down there now. The police are there. Do you know what is going on?"

"I'm about to find out. Third door, you say?"

"Oh, don't go now."

I told the girl I was on business and hurried down the stairs. As I reached the bottom of the stair, the crowd around the door to the one room stepped aside, and I saw four officers carrying a body in a yellow silk shirt and cherry red trousers. He had a butcher's knife stuck in the side of his neck.

Next I saw the third door open and two constables dragging a young lady, clothed in just her underwear, mind you, toward the door. She was dragging her feet, wiggling and struggling all over the place, and screaming, "I didn't do it."

Inspector Nickleby was there now. He said, "Quiet, Emma. We've got you dead to rights."

I had found my girl.

****

Back in the taproom I told my story. "You see, Bliss House is not quite a home to a well-to-do family. It's more of a house of entertainment. And the girl is not quite a governess. She is more of an entertainer." They got my meaning.

Miss Peggotty wailed away some more. Clara sobbed. Duff paced. Dickens raised his eyebrows, shrugged his shoulders, finished his pint, got out of his chair, and said, "Well, at least she is alive. I have an appointment with my publisher. Good day!" He waved to Jane as he left. She saw him to the door, and I saw him hand her a few coins.

I wished I could have gone along with Mr. Dickens. I wanted to meet his publisher, and I couldn't stand all the bawling, neither. But I knew I wanted to write this story, and if I didn't stay on the job I wouldn't know how it ended. I was going to write it if it had a happy ending, or if it had a sad ending. Right now it looked like a sad ending.

Then, of a sudden, Duff stopped his pacing. "Blathers, let's go and see Inspector Nickleby."

****

Scotland Yard was within walking distance. Duff plopped along like some big bird from somewhere out in the Empire. Us English are proud of our Empire. Just yesterday I was reading in the newspaper (I read the paper every day now) how successful England has been spreading Christianity in heathen India, taking English ways to the far reaches of the earth.

Anyway, neither of us minded the walk. Duff always liked to walk. I remember that time we walked to Spitalfields and back. My feet were killing me.

We found Inspector Nickleby in an office above the old stables. I could still smell horses. This is where the Superintendent of the Metropolitan Police stabled Pincher, before he gave the fine animal to Duff and me.

"Blathers and Duff! Are you here to do some investigating? How is Pincher? Are you taking good care of him?"

"Ah, we had to put down poor Pincher a while back. He was quite old, you know."

"That's too bad. I know how fond you were of that horse. He was a doughty animal."

I, as usual, wanted to get down to business. "Inspector, we are here on behalf of a client. She is a person who has raised Emma Peggotty, or perhaps she goes by Emma Stride."

"Sweet Emma, yes. She told us her name was Emma Stride when we arrested her. She drove a knife into that lummox who guarded the brothel. She may have had a good reason, but if she did, she hasn't said what it is."

I said, "I heard her say she didn't do it."

"That's what she keeps saying, but there is evidence to say she did."

"That is why we are here," Duff said. "We want to know what the evidence is."

"Well, normally we aren't supposed to disclose such information, but, truth be told, I find it hard to believe she did it, too. I find it hard to believe she was in that place at all. If you two can do something to help prove her innocence, I'll be glad."

I always knew Nickleby as fair, but this was the first I'd seen of a soft spot. A good policeman usually won't let his feelings get in the way of his work, and Nickleby was a good policeman.

He explained why he arrested Emma, and Duff took notes.

It seems the other residents of the house told that Emma had given the gaudy, bald giant a difficult time. The man's name was Henry Gander. Several times Emma tried to run away, and Gander caught her. When she found she couldn't escape, she barricaded the door to her room. Gander forced his way in. When she was sent a client (and this is a most damaging piece of testimony) she took a butcher's knife to the client and threatened to cut away any part of his body he displayed. She was starting to cost the house money, so the madam, one Mrs. Bardell, was not unhappy to hear about the murder of Gander, as long as this troublesome girl got the blame.

"In addition to the other girl's testimony, and the fact that Emma had a butcher's knife, we have evidence she was planning another escape." Inspector Nickleby's men found a dress and shoes, of the type worn by some religious dissenters, in a clothes press at the end of the hall where Emma had her room. One of the girls had told Nickleby she saw a plain-dressed lady in the house a few hours before the murder. "The thought is that Emma was going to sneak out of the house in her disguise, and Gander caught her, so she stabbed him. There are no other suspects. Only Emma seems to have had a reason to kill the man."

I asked Nickleby, "Do you know a person named Colonel Granger?"

"I believe that is an alias of one of the most notorious procurers of young women for the trade in London. If he is a colonel, then I'm a saint. I think his real name is Granger Sikes. The Sikes family are involved in almost every kind of crime in London."

Duff said, "It looks like this Sikes fellow trapped poor Emma into the house, and even if she did knife Gander, she did so in trying to escape captivity. You can't call that murder, Inspector."

"No, I can't, but the law does. You see, we won't be able to get the girls to tell their story in court, and Mrs. Bardell has some very important clients. It will be difficult for us to even prove the house was a bordello. Mrs. Bardell will claim it is a refuge for young women who have no other place to live, like a YMCA for girls. She will blackmail some of her most important clients into supporting her assertions with sworn statements. They won't even have to appear in court. We've been through this before."

****

We asked to talk with Emma, but Nickleby said it was not possible; some silly rule about solicitors and barristers. We once again returned to report our findings to Clara and her sister. We also needed to figure a way to bring out the truth of why the young girl, or anyone, had stuck a knife into the giant whorehouse gatekeeper.

Most of the tears had dried up by the time we got back to the taproom. It was also time for a beverage. Barkis, himself, obliged. Miss Betsey stopped her bawling and put on a stern face. It seems, while we were gone, Miss Betsey had decided the proper thing to do was to disown the girl, now she had taken up an immoral life. "It's in her blood. Just like her mother, she is."

Duff told her, "Miss Peggotty, it is not true that the young girl is immoral. These people trapped her and held her hostage. Some have said she defended her honor with a butcher's knife."

I added, "And that's the reason the Peelers have her in gaol. The lout was stuck in the neck with her knife."

Duff corrected me. "Well, it was a knife like the one she had used to threaten a patron of the establishment. They haven't said it was the same knife. Unfortunately, according to the Inspector, there will be lies told about what really happened in that house. If there was only some way to get in there and find the truth."

"Right, the Inspector says the only ones will know what really happened is the other girls and, of course, the customers. None of them will talk, will they."

Barkis looked at Clara. She had a big grin on her pudgy face. Clara glanced at Duff. He was almost laughing, very unusual for Duff, and shaking his head from side to side. Barkis, himself, started to chuckle. He said, "Are we all thinking the same thing?"

I said, "What's going on?"

Clara shook her head. "No, no, it would be sinful. We don't want any sinning."

Duff said, "Clara, there's sinning goes on every day, some of it even by Blathers."

Barkis, himself, said, "Clara, my dear, God will forgive anything if it is for a righteous cause."

Clara said, "Maybe, my dear, but will he do it?"

Duff said, "I think he would do it without a righteous cause."

Barkis said, "It will be expensive. That place must only have high-paying customers."

Duff said, "Yes, we will have to dress him up. That will cost, too, but don't worry about the costs."

Chapter Two
The Second Visit

That evening, about eight, I found myself dressed like the finest East End toff, complete with a silk top hat. Once again I knocked on the door of the house in St. John's Wood.

"Good evening, sir. What brings you to my door?"

"Good evening, madam. I should like to be entertained."

"I am afraid I know you not. Why do you think there is entertainment here?"

I had my story ready. "I was given your name by a friend. I have long been away in the Foreign Service. I was recently called back for a consultation. A gentleman in that agency, whose name I would prefer not to mention, suggested I stop at your door. He said I should ask for Kit. You do have an entertainer by that name, do you not?"

"Why, we do, indeed. And she is available this evening; how fortunate for you. Please come in. Please leave ten pounds on the hall table."

****

"It cost me ten quid. That's more than I spend in a month. And these clothes must have cost plenty. Who's standing the cost?"

Duff and I were in our room upstairs in the Black

Lion. Duff suggested we meet there after my "field investigation" in case there were details unsuitable for a lady's ear.

"We are paying the expenses this time. Mr. and Mrs. Barkis have been very good to us, and we owe them this favor. I'm sure you understand."

"Maybe we do, and maybe they don't have the cash to pay for my duds and my, should we say, research costs, but where are we getting the money?"

"Lady Peel has been very generous to us. The Iron Duke and Sir Robert have also arranged for us to be paid a sizable reward from the government for our efforts in uncovering the activities of the Maltese Cross Gang."

"I haven't seen any money. You know I am now studying mathematics with Miss Alice, and I can tell if you aren't being fair with me."

"So, you have gotten over your emotions concerning Miss Martin. That's good."

"Don't change the subject. Where is the money?"

"Blathers, after all these years, don't you trust me?"

"I just asked a simple question. Where is the money?"

"You know, you are starting to age."

"Where is the money?"

"I'm trying to tell you."

"Just tell me, then."

"If you would stop yelling, I would."

"I'm not yelling. You are."

The door flung open and Barkis, himself, stood there with his hands on his hips. "Stop, both of you! You're upsetting the ladies."

"All I want to know is where is the money?"

"I am trying to tell him I have it invested for our retirement."

"Right! Well, why didn't you say so?"

Barkis said, "Both of you, downstairs. We all want to know what was discovered at Bliss House."

****

I began my report to ladies and gents alike. If they heard something that made them blush, so be it.

"I was admitted to the house. Kit seemed to recognize me, but she couldn't remember where she'd seen me afore. Of course, when she saw me on the day of the killing I was dressed much different. Duff, do you think it would have cost less than ten quid if I was dressed like I usually am?"

"I don't think you would have been admitted at all."

"Why not? That Gander fellow told me to come back later. He would have let me in."

"Maybe he thought you were delivering something. Anyway, the disguise worked. Now, what did you find out?"

"Right. I'll skip some of the details, but Kit and I had a good talk, off and on."

"So to speak," Barkis said. Clara gave him a look that said he should keep quiet.

"Here's what she told me. This Colonel Granger—Nickleby says his real name is Granger Sikes—and Mrs. Bardell own the house. Gander was their muscle man. Colonel Granger would lure young girls just arrived in London to the house. Gander would keep them there. After a few weeks of beatings, most would stay. No telling what happened to those that didn't. Kit tells me, quite confidentially, if you please, Emma was a fighter. First time Gander comes her way, she kicks him where it hurts most, if you ladies will excuse the way I put it, and Gander goes away all doubled over. After that she found the knife, and Gander was afraid to go near her. None of the customers wanted a thing to do with her either, but there was one fellow who would visit her on the sly."

Duff asked, "What fellow is that?"

"Now that's just the thing. Kit says the first time he comes to the house he asks for Emma. He goes up and stays awhile, then comes down and asks for his money back. Says that Emma wouldn't cooperate. Kit saw the fellow and says, just like me, he looks kind of familiar."

Barkis said, "I'm bettin' that most lads look familiar to Kit." Clara hit him on the shoulder with a wooden spoon.

I went on, "She said, too, that Mrs. Bardell and Granger were glad to be rid of Emma, for all the trouble she caused. They were probably not sorry to lose Gander, either. Kit says she thinks he knew too much about the way the house was run."

Miss Betsey was on her feet. "The cads! I'll have the police down on them. Trying to ruin my sweet Emma! I don't care what her mother was like. She's an innocent girl."

I said, "I'm afraid you won't get much help from the police. It is highly likely that police officials are customers there."

Duff said, "Blathers, do you remember those girls Caddy Quale obtained to act in our little play for Sir Percy Wesley?"

"Right, you mean Nell and Betty."

"Yes, those two. Do you know how to contact them? Maybe they can be of some help."

"I might."

****

Now, you have to understand, Nell and Betty deal with a different kind of fellows than the girls in St. John's Wood. Out there was all barons and ministers and Knights of the Garter and all. Nell and Betty charged less. The two of them, and they quite often worked as a twosome, would spend a week with you for ten quid. Their customers are, well, like them newspaper lads what were with Mr. Dickens when we caught Sir Percy with, shall we say, his trousers down. Oh, I remember that scene well. Those ladies of the Vice Society beating on Sir Percy and ogling at his privates. And every time he tried to yank up his pants they would hit him again and take a good look for themselves.

Anyway, because Duff thought it might be helpful, I was, just by luck, mind you, able to locate the girls. They were very helpful, and when they found out I had paid ten pounds to interview Kit, they said they wouldn't charge me for the time with them, even though, as they pointed out, since there were two of them, I would, no doubt, receive twice the satisfaction.

After engaging in the usual polite activities, I asked the girls, "Now, ladies, what can you tell me about Bliss House and the folks that run it?"

Nell said, "Blathers, you know we isn't in the same game as them out there."

Betty said, "Right you are. We ain't had no peer o' the realm in over five years."

Nell said, "But we has heard o' that rat Granger

Sikes. He hangs around the train stations, you know, and when he sees a likely girl get off the train wearin' country duds, he strikes. Lot's o' girls make the mistake o' fallin' fer his line."

Betty said, "I almost made that same mistake meself." She had a squeaky little voice.

Nell said, "It's a shame he ain't in gaol. Them toffs is so anxious to have a little bit o' fun, they keeps a cad like that from being sent away."

Betty said, "Them fools doesn't know what a good time they might has wi' the two o' us. And for a lot less money."

I once again explained my problem to the ladies. "Well, now, girls, you see the difficulty. The girls there won't talk, and, for sure, the customers won't talk. I would go back as a customer, but it's so expensive, and I'm getting tired."

Nell and Betty said together, "Use the tradesmen's entrance."

Chapter Three
The Third Visit

The people in the great houses of London are very fussy about who comes through their front door. They all have someone who has the job of, you might say, guarding the door so that only the best people are let in. In most places, the butler does it. At the house in St. John's Wood, Henry Gander did the guarding, but since he was gone, Mrs. Bardell had taken up the task. Of course, the interesting thing is that the back door receives little attention. I suppose it's Cook's responsibility there, since that's who I met when I went in the tradesmen's entrance of Mrs. Bardell's place.

I had gone back to the Black Lion to get Duff to help me get into the house. He was helpful, but by the time we had agreed on a plan, as usual I was the one doing the going in. The way it worked was this.

Barkis took me and five cases of Madeira to the back of the house. I rang the bell and someone called out, "Come in, come in. I'm too busy now to get the door."

I went in and said, "I have a delivery."

"All deliveries should be made before eleven o'clock, don't ya know." After eleven o'clock it was Cook's job to mash the potatoes, overcook the meat, and see that the beer and wine were kept warm. She also napped from time to time.

"This is a special. Five cases of Madeira for a Mr. Gander."

"Sure, keep them girls a little snapped, and they won't mind making a living on their backs. Does ya know where it goes?"

"I don't. Should I take it to Mr. Gander?"

"Mr. Gander is… That is, he isn't with us any longer. Just put them in the small room next to the parlor. You'll see the empty bottles stored there."

Duff had insisted we use full cases of wine, should anyone want to inspect the delivery. I took the full cases in and found the empty bottles and cases as Cook said I would. We had bought the wine from Barkis at a discount, and he threw in free delivery with his cart, but it still seemed a shame to waste all this fine beverage by leaving it there. I needed to think about that. First though, I needed to look around and see what I could see. As I turned from the storage room, a cute young girl, perhaps eighteen, came into the room with a feather duster. "Hello, there," she said. "I haven't seen you around afore."

I said, "Have some Madeira, my dear?"

****

"I'm off in just a quarter hour. My room is over the stables in the back. Just go in. I'll be along."

As I hauled the empty bottles to Barkis' cart, I included one full carton of wine, to share with my new friend. "Barkis, lad, you go on back to the inn. Don't fret about me. I'll find my way home." The girl came along as promised. We were all wrong about who we needed to talk to about the doings in the house. Maids know more than anyone about what's going on in any house. I'll tell all that she told me later on, in the taproom in the Black Lion. Right now, all I can say is, I know why they give the girls of the house all that Madeira.

****

It was the next day afore I was able to meet with Duff and the others. "A wee bit of brandy, please, Clara, my dear. Seems I have upset my stomach in the line of duty."

"Right away, Mr. Blathers. You poor lad. You look like you haven't had a wink for days."

"Oh, I've slept. It just didn't help. Them, I mean those, sweet wines aren't good for the head. But, sweet wines do help the mouth to work, that is, the mouth of a lady at the brothel." I sipped my brandy and said, "I'll tell what I found out in the room above the stable."

"Before you begin," Duff said, "Please tell us where exactly you have been, and what you have been doing since yesterday."

"I've been from heaven to hell, and I'm not quite back from hell. What I did along the way I'm saving for the book I'm going to write. They tell me that a good bawdy tale helps to sell books."

Here I must apologize to the reader. The publisher wouldn't let me describe what actually happened between the maid and me as we consumed the wine. All he would let me say is that the maid was better company than Kit and was free, except for the wine.

I saw Barkis' eyes go wide, and Clara hit him with the wooden spoon again. Miss Betsey covered her eyes so she wouldn't hear anything she shouldn't. "Now, now, folks, all I'm going to do is tell what the girl told me. If you want more, you'll have to read the book.

After we got to know each other better…"

The spoon smacked Barkis before he could make one of his smart remarks.

I began again. "After we became acquainted, I asked the girl why it is she could just take the afternoon off."

"She said she could come and go as she pleased. Cook was supposed to watch the door, but she is so fat and lazy everyone comes and goes without her knowing. She likened as how I just walked out with the wine.

"Well, she was right. Cook was asleep at her table when I took out the empty bottles and the full case. To cut to the important thing, though it took me some time afore I found this out, there was a delivery man that would visit with Emma each time he made a delivery. He brought baked goods to the house every day, and would sneak to Emma's room every time. She says he would stay about an hour and then sneak out through the back door."

Duff asked, "What about Gander? If he was guarding the girls, wouldn't he be watching the back door?"

"She said there was a rule. The girls had to stay out of the back of the house. Gander would only go back there if one of them did. He didn't know how the care of the house was done, so even if he saw Emma's visitor on the stair, he wouldn't give it a thought."

Miss Betsey jumped to a conclusion. "So this strange chap must have been the one that did the stabbing."

"Not necessarily. There was also an odd woman spotted. You recall the lady's clothes found in the closet. Well, my friend, the maid, she is sure Emma never wore them. She thinks a woman sneaked in disguised in those clothes. She is certain she saw the lady in the front hall the day Gander was stuck in the neck."

Duff said, "So another possible suspect."

"More than a suspect. My friend says she has seen the woman waiting around the back of the house since the killing. She hasn't tried to go in, but she's watching."

Duff had a suggestion. "Then, why don't you go back to Bliss House and see if you can spot her."

Chapter Four
The Fourth Visit

Back I went again. Duff thought he was clever, convincing me to make another trip to St. John's Wood. I made like he pushed me against my will, but I was happy for another opportunity to see my friend the maid. By the way, I haven't told you her name. It's Daisy. She is as sweet and fresh as the daisy in the field at sunrise.

I waited behind the stable until I saw her leave the main house and go to her room. I said, "Ah, my dear, how are you this fine day?"

She said, "Quiet, Look over there."

There she was in a plain gray, homespun frock with a matching bonnet. She was watching the house and watching Daisy and me, as well.

"She comes every day. She's always here when the baker's man comes, but she doesn't let him see her. She ducks behind that there hedge when he's around."

"Let's go to your room and see what she does." When we got there, sweet Daisy couldn't wait to give me a kiss. We were standing right in front of the window, and I know the mysterious woman saw us because, when I glanced in her direction, it looked like she might be sneering at us. I say, might be, because the bonnet covered her face in a shadow.

I pulled my sweet girl back into the room where we could still see the woman but she couldn't see us. "When does the baker's man come?"

"Not for another half hour at least."

"Well, how will we spend the time?"

****

Let me just say, at this point, a half hour isn't much time at all. Make of that what you will. No matter, my very lovely friend and I were in a position to view his arrival, standing just back from the window, I mean.

Daisy said, "Here he comes with the tarts for the tarts. Now, just watch what she does." And the woman did. She huddled behind the shrubs so as he wouldn't see her. The man was quite ordinary, thin, you might say, like a willow branch. He was probably between thirty-five and forty. He had a beard, neatly trimmed, but covering most of his face. You know, he looked somewhat familiar to me. "Where have I seen that man before? Well, I'll have to think about that."

And another thing. The strange woman, now, she looked familiar, as well. I thought my mind was playing tricks on me.

It was time for me to get my head cleared, so I said to Daisy, "Well, I had best be on my way."

Daisy said, "Why don't you stay?"

I said, "For the whole day?"

She said, "For as long as you may."

****

The next day I sent a note to Duff, by way of a boy on the street. I was sure it would get there because I told the lad Duff would pay him when he delivered it safely. In the note I told Duff I would be missing for a few days, as I was working on a watch of suspects in our case. I also told him to be generous paying the boy. I said I thought his name was Joe. That always got Duff to loose the pocketbook strings a wee bit.

So, after getting that business done, I went back to Daisy's room. She was cleaning at the house. I had asked her to hang around until the baker's man came with his goods. Maybe she could strike up a conversation with him and find out his name or something.

She's a clever girl, my Daisy. She was in the yard just as he was leaving after delivering his goods. As he approached her she started toward him, and, at just the right moment, she tripped. He caught her as she fell forward. He didn't let go right away, and she didn't try to pull loose. I figured maybe I shouldn't have sent my note. I guess I was a little green-eyed, as they say.

But I wasn't the only jealous one. From where I was standing, I could see the strange woman. She was livid, still hiding, but waving her arms in the air and tugging at her bonnet. She looked like a crazy lady.

Finally, after some time passed, Daisy regained her footing. It looked like she thanked the fellow for keeping her from falling, and they spoke a few words. He tipped his flat cap at her, and she went into the house. She wasn't there long when she came back out, carrying something wrapped in paper, and walked toward her room.

The door opened and she said, "Why, Blathers, aren't you just sitting there with your arms folded over your chest."

"It looked like you sure enjoyed yourself with that fellow."

"Now, my dear, that was just playacting, but this

isn't."

It wasn't only a few minutes afore she had me convinced she was only playing with the other lad. Afterwards, we ate the two pastries she had smuggled out of the kitchen. Then I asked, "Right, now, what did you find out? Did he tell you his name? Do you know where he lives?"

"I know he has very strong arms."

"How could a scrawny fellow like that have strong arms?"

"They felt good around me." Daisy grinned. "But of course not as strong and comfortable as yours."

"Now, stop this nonsense and tell me what it is you learned."

"His name is Jack. I asked him about his visits with Emma. He said he knew her. She was a customer at the bakery when first she was in London. He saw her here again when he was making his delivery. She asked for help to get out. They had a plan what was just about ready when the killing happened."

"You found out a bit for such a short time."

"I'll be finding out more. I'll be meeting him tomorrow when he's making his delivery."

"I don't like that. It could be dangerous."

"Oh, Blathers, you've nothing to worry about. I'm doing this for you. You can watch from this here room. Of course, I may have to kiss him to loosen his lips."

"Right, as long as his lips are the only thing you loosen. I'll be watching."

"By the way, was the woman watching while I was chatting up Jack?"

"She was, and as soon as he touched you she went wild. I think she might be one of them crazy ladies."

The crazy lady disappeared right after the baker's man left. But she was back again soon after teatime, and she seemed to be looking toward Daisy's room. She was there just a short time, and then she disappeared again.

****

The next day I slept late. This business of keeping watch on a place is tiring work. By the time I got awake, Daisy was off to the main house. She worked the most in the morning, when Cook was most awake. By afternoon, Cook was sleeping so much she didn't know where my Daisy was. Anyway, Daisy says that keeping the place neat is only part-time work. She will meet the pastry man about half ten, tell me all she's found out over a noon meal, and then we will spend the afternoon trying to make sense out of the clues we have.

I made myself some tea on a little stove in the corner of the room and was sipping it as Jack, the baker's man, made his delivery. The scene was a repeat of the previous day, except Daisy didn't have to fall down. There was a bench in a circle around a big oak tree standing between the house and the stable. She and Jack sat on the side of the tree away from the house. Someone looking from there couldn't see them, but I had a perfect view. She took the fellow's hand in hers and looked into his eyes like he was the only person on earth. For such a young girl she certainly knew how to handle people, well, men anyway.

Of course, the crazy lady was behind the bush. I was watching Daisy so close like, I almost forgot to watch for her. She was acting saner today, very calm. She moved from her regular place behind the bushes to another old tree out in the yard. She stood so Daisy and Jack couldn't see her. Then, as I was watching, she stepped out from behind the tree. She raised her arm. She held a pistol in her hand. I yelled, "Daisy, duck!" A bullet lodged itself in the tree just over Daisy's right shoulder.

Daisy fell to the ground, and Jack jumped behind the tree. It's a good show the bullet missed over Daisy's right shoulder, because Jack was sitting very close on her left. By the time I looked back, the crazy lady, now I was certain, very crazy, was gone. Jack helped Daisy to her feet, saw she wasn't hurt, made a little bow, and ran off in the direction where the shooter had been. I was now in the yard, holding my girl as close as possible. Cook yelled out, "Keep all that noise down out there, I'm workin' in here, don't ya know."

****

"I didn't think you were right when you said it might be dangerous to meet the fellow. I thought you were just a wee bit jealous."

"Thank the Lord you weren't hurt. I believe I've become quite fond of you."

"Ah, you needn't worry, my sweet. Where I come from, being shot at happens often. But, you know, I am quite fond of you, as well."

We returned to the room and were clinging to each other when there was a knock at the door. I pushed Daisy into a front corner of the room, where whoever was at the door couldn't see her. Knowing a bullet can go right through wood, I stepped to one side and said, "Who is it?"

"Blathers, It's me. Open up."

Duff came wobbling in, his long gangly legs

stepping high, and his head bobbing up and down on his long neck.

"How did you find me?" I asked.

"I am a detective, you know."

"Don't be a smart mouth. How did you find me?"

"I received your note and gave that fine young lad, Joe, several coins for his trouble. Then I started to wonder about your situation. Perhaps the note was a fraud, and you were in some sort of difficulty. I thought it would only be right for me to investigate, so I lingered outside the house to see if I could see you. The messenger boy told me you gave him the note on a street near St. John's Wood. When I heard the shot, I came behind the house to see what had happened. I saw you and this young lady enter this building, and here I am. Now, what is going on?"

"This is Daisy."

"How do you do, Daisy. Are you one of the, ah, staff at the house?"

"Yes, I work at the house." Daisy had a gleam in her eye. "I am one of the most important members of staff, as you put it."

"Well, I see. And is Mr. Blathers one of your customers?" Without waiting for an answer, Duff turned to me. "Blathers, I thought we had agreed we would limit certain expenses in this case."

I wanted to tell Duff the truth, but Daisy answered. "Don't worry about the expense, Mr. Duff. I have found Mr. Blathers to be such an excellent, well, you know, that I'm not going to charge him a thing."

She had my skinny partner all red in the face. He was squirming and staring at the floor, not able to say a thing more.

Both me and Daisy were chuckling. I said, "Look, Duff, you have it all wrong. Daisy is not what you think. She's the girl of all work at the house. This is her room. She doesn't have a room in the house. She was kidding you. She's quite a kidder, is my Daisy."

"Your Daisy? This is more serious than I thought. Well, we'll talk about it later. Now, tell me about what has developed with our case. Who got shot?"

I told Duff all there was to know about Jack, Emma's visitor, and the crazy one what took a shot at Daisy, or maybe it was a shot at Jack. "I for one would say those two are mixed up in this killing some way. By the way, did I mention I had a strange feeling I had seen both of them before?"

Duff said, "Perhaps I should wait around and see if I recognize either of them. You know, with my mind's eye, I have a way of remembering things many people forget."

"Right, but I don't think either of them will be back again today, so you can go, and come back tomorrow."

Daisy agreed wholeheartedly. "Yes, Mr. Duff, you don't want to waste all day hanging around here, now, do you?"

Duff said to Daisy, "Well, I could do some investigating. Blathers usually does our outside work, but if he, and I guess you, are watching the house, I guess I understand. Tell me, do you know where the bakery is? I could go by, make a small purchase, and see what I can see."

"That is a good idea, Mr. Duff. Wait right here. I'll run up the house and find out for you."

"Very good, and when would it be a good time for me to stop back here to discuss any information I get?"

Daisy looked at me and nodded. I said, "Tomorrow morning about ten will be just the time. We expect the bakery man will make his usual delivery about that time, and we can see what happens then. Be sure to try the lemon tarts at the bakery. We've found them to be lovely."

****

After Duff left to do his investigation, Daisy got some food from the house along with a bottle of wine. We enjoyed a marvelous lunch. We were having a quiet afternoon, which we both deserved because of the excitement of the morning, when, just before teatime, there was banging on the door again. We were both still skittish, so we immediately jumped to our feet. I made sure Daisy was out of sight of the door and asked who was there, standing away from the line of fire, to be sure.

"It's me. I've been to the bakery. Let me in. I must talk with you."

I looked at Daisy. All she was wearing was a beautiful smile. "Right, give me a minute. The door seems to be stuck." I rattled the knob while I made sure the lock was in place.

"Let me try." Duff pushed and shoved. Thank goodness the lock held while both Daisy and I made ourselves presentable.

We finally opened the door. "Duff, I don't know what happened. The lock must have stuck."

"Well, you certainly mussed your hair trying to open it."

"Never you mind. I thought you were going to wait till tomorrow to come back."

"Obviously!"

"Right, then what are you doing here now?"

"As I was purchasing my lemon tart, the delivery man returned from his rounds. I think I know who he is."

"Well, who is it, then?"

"I'm not positive, because it was so long ago, and I really only had a fleeting glance of him."

"Well, who do you think it is?"

"I think you thought you recognized him because he looks very much like his father."

"Like whose father?"

"Why…"

More banging on the door.

"Who's there?" Both Daisy and Duff darted for out-of-the-way corners.

"It's Jack Squod. I need your help."

****

The baker's man was Jack Squod, son of the former owner of the Black Lion and fugitive, wanted for the murder of Lizabeth Stride. I don't know why Duff wouldn't tell me that. Sometimes he is so strange.

I yanked the door open, grabbed Squod by the shoulder, spun him around, and put a hammerlock on him. "Squod, I'm arresting you for murder."

"Please, Mr. Blathers, hear what I have to say. I desperately need help. It's Jane. She has gone mad again, but this time she has the child. The child is in grave danger."

Duff said, "Blathers, let him go. Let's hear his story." He pushed a wooden chair up against the wall, and I shoved Squod into it.

"Right, now, let's have it."

"It's Jane, Jane from the Black Lion. You know

her. She has gone completely mad this time. I've always been able to quiet her in the past, but this time she ran out of the house and took our daughter with her. I saw you at the bakery, Mr. Duff. I knew you recognized me. I went home to ask Jane what she thought we should do. She shot at me again with the gun, grabbed Dora, and ran. She's holed up now in the house."

Duff asked, "The house! What house?"

"Bliss House! She has the gun. She said she was going to kill all the whores."

I asked, "Will she do it?"

"I'm afraid she will, and it won't be the first time."

****

There was no time to waste. "Daisy, my love, you stay right here, out of harm's way. Come on, Duff. I've been in the house and know my way around. Let's see what the situation is. Squod, you sit yourself down and don't move. I'm still not sure about you."

Duff said, "Perhaps I should stay here and watch Squod."

"Daisy will do that. Come on."

We ran from the stables to the tradesmen's entrance and peeked in. Cook was snoring away. We could hear a commotion further on in the house. I signaled to Duff to be quiet. I cracked the heavy door that separated the back of the house from the business section. I could see Mrs. Bardell cowering on a stuffed chair. Behind her, along the wall, five almost naked women huddled together. There was sweet, peaches and cream, lovely, buxom Jane. But her face looked diabolical, and she was waving a pistol in her right hand. Next to her was a young girl of about thirteen.

Jane held her by the hair with her left hand. Well, we now knew the situation. I let the door close slowly.

"Duff you go around to the front door. You'll find a huge doorknocker. Bang it as hard as you can, and don't stop till someone opens the door." Duff went out, and it was only a wee bit till I heard the knocking. It was loud, for sure. Too loud, because Cook woke up.

"What's all the noise? Where is that Gander ta answer the door? Oh, yeah, I forgot. And who are you? Get out of my way. A body can't get any work done with all the goings on around here." She pushed through the door into the front of the house. The knocking continued.

Jane spun around and fired. She missed her target, but Cook fainted and crumpled to the floor. Mrs. Bardell and the girls all stayed right where they were. I noticed that the gun was a six-shooting revolver. That was three shots gone. Three to go, if she hadn't reloaded since firing two shots this morning. The knocking continued.

I pushed the door open and jumped behind the wall, shouting, "Answer the door." The fourth bullet went into the kitchen somewhere. I thought I heard a frying pan ring out. The knocking continued. I retreated into the kitchen. The frying pan gave me an idea. There was some rope in the pantry. I tied it to one pan. I set it on the table and piled several other pots on top of it. I went back to the door, flung it open again, jumped to one side and yanked the rope. A great crash, and another shot. "One to go." The knocking continued.

I peeked once more at the scene in the parlor. The knocking from the front and the noises from the kitchen were agitating Jane. She threw young Dora in among the girls. "Get o'er there with them whores. You be as bad as any of 'em. Flirtin' wi' your own dad. You're all occasions o' sin. Ya lead all men inta temptation. I'll rid London o' ya blackhearted hussies."

She waved the gun back and forth, from the front door to the kitchen door. Each time the pistol would pass the girls, they would cringe and huddle together. Kit took Dora and put the poor girl behind her. The knocking went on.

Jack Squod and Daisy appeared in the kitchen behind me. "I couldn't stop him coming down when we heard the shots," Daisy explained.

"Never mind. Just get to one side there so you don't get shot."

Jack pushed me away and ran toward the front room. He pushed the door open wide. "Jane, stop before you kill someone else. This has to stop here and now. Give me the gun."

The knocking had stopped.

Jane pointed the gun directly at Jack's heart. "Jack, always fallin' in wi' the tarts. You is a weak one, you is. I'll deliver ya from evil."

Duff jumped on her back, and the sixth bullet went into the floor.

****

The incident at Bliss House accomplished what all the churches, anti-vice committees, and police had been unable to do. Bliss House went out of business. The Metropolitan Police carted Jane away. Young Jerry Cruncher was part of the force that finally responded to reports of gunfire in the neighborhood.

Daisy packed her bits and pieces, and we stopped to drop them off at my rooms on our way to the Black

Lion. Duff had gone off to visit Inspector Nickleby and get Emma let go. They were both in the taproom of the old inn when we got there. Of course Clara and her sister and Barkis, himself, were present. I was, however, surprised to see Jack Squod and young Dora among the gathering.

Duff said, “Blathers, now that you are here, Jack will tell his story.”

“Not till my Daisy and I have some refreshment. By the way, Duff, how did you get into the front room behind Jane?”

“I kept knocking until my arm got tired. Then I tried the door. It wasn’t locked, so I just went in, and there I was just in time.”

Barkis, himself, said, “I’ll say just in time,” as he did the honors, brandy and a pint for me, a large Madeira for Daisy. Everyone now had a beverage, and Squod began.

“You will recall when you detectives thought I murdered Liz Stride. It wasn’t me, but I suspected it was Jane. We had been lovers for some time. She, however, was unable to control her jealousy. She swore to me it wasn’t her did the killing, and she took me in. We have been living together all these years, right here in this neighborhood. When she went to care for her sick aunt, that’s when Dora was born.

“I felt she was going to be all right when she started going to church. She would dress up in one of her plain smocks and bonnet every Sunday and be gone the whole day. As it turned out, church only made her worse. When I befriended Emma and tried to help her out of her deplorable situation, well, you saw what happened. She tried to get at Emma with her knife, but the bodyguard stopped her. She left her knife in his neck. I think that's why she got the gun."

Duff said, "So you are sure Jane was the murderer of Lizabeth Stride?"

"There is no question about it. I'm quite sure she was also responsible for a number of other killings. Sometimes she would tell me she had to work in the evening. The next day, one of her smocks would be put out to dry and there would be talk of another killing."

It was a sad story, with an even sadder ending. Later that day Inspector Nickleby stopped by the inn to tell us Jane had hung herself with the cord she used to suspend a cross around her neck.

Author's Note

The other authors of the stories that appear in this book have selected me to write this note because, as the anonymous author of the first story has said, I "talk with the reader." He is anonymous because he is a friend of Mr. Dickens. He said that he didn't want Dickens to know he wrote the story because he didn't want his relationship with his friend to turn "dark and stormy."

As it turned out, Mr. Dickens' publisher was "too involved with other projects at this time" to take on our book. Fortunately, our anonymous author had publishing friends.

By the way, if you are familiar with any of Mr. Dickens' work, you will notice some of the characters, including me and Duff, are in his stories. He has a lot of the names mixed up with other characters, and he doesn't describe some at all like they are. For example, me and Duff are in *Oliver Twist*. He doesn't even come close to describing me like I am. And poor Duff, he makes Duff look like a dunce with no personality. Well, we won't talk about his personality, but you can see from our stories that he is no dummy. But I guess we can forgive Mr. Dickens. After all, his stories are fiction.

A word about the author...

Mike is retired from a successful career in the insurance business. He now lives with his wife in the beautiful Finger Lakes region of New York. Unfortunately, because of allergies, there are no pets.

Thank you for purchasing
this publication of The Wild Rose Press, Inc.

If you enjoyed the story, we would appreciate your letting others know by leaving a review.

For other wonderful stories,
please visit our on-line bookstore at
www.thewildrosepress.com.

For questions or more information
contact us at
info@thewildrosepress.com.

The Wild Rose Press, Inc.
www.thewildrosepress.com

Stay current with The Wild Rose Press, Inc.

Like us on Facebook

https://www.facebook.com/TheWildRosePress

And Follow us on Twitter
https://twitter.com/WildRosePress